The Marshal's Bride

Courtney
always
dream big!!
love Maxine Douglas

MAXINE DOUGLAS

The Marshal's Bride
by Maxine Douglas

Copyright 2017 © D.H. Fritter
All Rights Reserved

Cover Layout by Maria Connor
Edited by Maria Connor
Print Layout by D.H. Fritter

Manufactured in the United States of America

Second Edition June 2017
First Edition May 2017
ISBN-10: 154666534X
ISBN-13: 978-1546665342

DEDICATION

To the men and women who dared to settle in what is now known as Oklahoma.

To my husband who will always have my heart no matter what path we travel down

ACKNOWLEDGMENTS

My heartfelt thanks to Patricia Cummingham at the Grady County Historical Museum in Chickasha, Oklahoma. Thank you for allowing me to spend hours in the museum going through materials you gathered for me on Fred, Indian Territory while you made preparations for the 150 Anniversary of the Chisholm Trail.

To Mark Rathe, President of the Chickasha Chamber of Commerce, for planting the seed of a series for the 150th Anniversary of The Chisholm Trail.

To my friend Callie Hutton for always being the voice of encouragement to drive me in the right direction.

AUTHOR NOTE

According to *Chronicles of Oklahoma*, Vol. 12, No. 4, December, 1934, pg. 449, Fred, Indian Territory, was originally on the north bank of the Washita River before moving south of the river to the Stage Road and near the Little Washita River in 1881. For purposes of my story I have used the former site of Fred, Indian Territory, which eventually became known as Old Fred.

As for the historical figures of Deputy U.S. Marshal Bass Reeves and the Jesse Evans Gang, I have placed them in Fred, Indian Territory (Oklahoma), in the late summer of 1877. It is likely Reeves may have been in Fred at that time, but highly unlikely that the Jesse Evans Gang was. The Jesse Evans gang was a lesser known gang who cattle rustled and robbed banks in New Mexico.

CHAPTER ONE

Dodge City
1877

"She's got to be there, Spade. Her telegram was quite clear." Marshal Gabe Hawkins sat on his black gelding at the corner of the jail, watching as the train steamed into Dodge City. The hot steel wheels hissed and screeched to a halt along the iron rails, causing sparks to fly in the air. The steam from the engine's smokestack finally cleared and the passengers began to disembark, one by one.

The visitors to Dodge City stepped onto the platform. After what he'd said all these years about not being in the market for a family, Gabe stared at a curvy woman getting off the train from Kansas City with his friend, Logan. *What the heck was I thinking? And what is Logan doing back from his trip to clear Rose?*

The raids his southern unit took part in sickened him as much today as it did at the height of the War Between the States. A West Point cadet thrown into the war, Gabe had seen more senseless killing than he ever wanted to see again. After families like his were torn apart by either death or choosing opposite sides, he'd made a promise to himself to never put someone he loved into that situation.

Instead he took an oath, pinned on a star, and headed west to protect the citizens trying to recover after the devastation. And that oath kept Gabe from losing his heart to a woman and settling down with a family. That is, until he realized his role as marshal wasn't enough. He didn't want to spend the rest of his days alone. That he wanted a woman to come home to. So, he made the decision to resign from being a lawman, sent an advertisement for a bride, and aimed to live the rest of his days in peace.

And now hopefully she was standing on the depot platform. The woman standing next to Dodge City's very own Pinkerton Agent Logan Granger in animated conversation had to be his bride. The curvy woman in the neat dress, brown hair highlighted with a streak of silver pulled back into a bun under her hat, appeared to match the photograph he'd received a month ago. His heart raced like a stampede of longhorn. Only one way to find out if Miss Abigail Johnson had indeed arrived on time.

"If she's ours, Spade, I'd better go stake a claim on her before someone else does." He checked his vest for the ring and marriage license then patted the black gelding's neck and took a deep breath. "At least I know Logan is spoken for."

His horse stomped a foot. Gabe's heart pounded. His hands were clammy. God help the people of Dodge if for any reason he had to draw his gun. The pearl-handled grip would surely slip right out of his hand. Then he'd either be lying up in Doc Elliott's, bleeding all over the place, or stretched out at the undertaker's.

Neither option appealed to Gabe. And he was sure his new bride wouldn't appreciate it either.

"Logan!" Stetson pulled down low, Gabe spurred his horse and trotted up next to the train depot. Dismounting, he tipped his hat and smiled, immediately recognizing the woman from the photograph he'd received, "Ma'am."

"Marshal Gabe Hawkins meet—"

"Miss Abigail Johnson." Gabe smiled, stepping close enough to get a faint whiff of lavender. "I trust your trip was uneventful."

"Mr. Hawkins, it's nice to finally meet you." Abigail's voice was soft and full of nervous laughter. "It was quite the spectacle, seeing wild buffalo grazing out in the open and an Indian every now and again."

"You know each other?" Logan whistled, then chuckled. "Don't tell me you've—"

"We've been corresponding for several weeks." Gabe tore his gaze from Abigail, turning a scowl onto his friend. He wasn't ready to tell Logan the reasons he'd sent for a mail-order bride, and he suspected Abigail hadn't said anything as well.

Logan raised an eyebrow then waved some documents in the air. "I'm on my way over to the jail now to bring Rose some news regarding the trumped-up charges against her. As luck would have it, Miss Johnson was on her way to Dodge City to deliver the court documents in person. She recognized me in Topeka and has saved me a trip north. Miss Johnson, will Rose and I see you later for dinner? You know she'll skin me alive if I don't insist."

Abigail smiled, nodding her head. "By all means, there is so much Rose and I have to catch up on since she left Wisconsin to marry you. Go give her the good news I brought from your superior and take her home.

I'm sure the marshal will make sure I find my way to the hotel." She looked at Gabe for a moment then lowered her lashes.

The flirtatious gesture set his heart to pounding. Abigail's letters had shown her to be smart, witty, and a bit headstrong. His decision to take a wife seemed to be proving advantageous. "I'd be honored, Miss Johnson. I'll have your bags sent over to the Dodge House. In the meantime, how about a sundae at Etta May's after a long, dusty train ride?" Gabe pulled his hat from his head, then swept his hand through unruly curls to tame them back.

Her cheeks blushed a pretty rose petal pink, bringing a youthfulness to her wise brown eyes. "I've already taken care of my bags, but the sundae sounds heavenly. Do you mind giving me a chance to freshen up before sitting down for a good conversation?"

"Of course not. Take all the time you need. I agree we need a chance to talk and get to know each other a bit more, if that would be fine with you." Gabe reached out, placing a hand lightly on her lower back. She stood a good five to six inches shorter than his six-foot frame yet they seemed completely suited to each other as they strolled across the street over to the Dodge House, Spade trailing behind.

"Thank you, Mr. Hawkins. I won't be but a few minutes. I had already requested a room when I had my bags sent over." Abigail stepped from his touch and turned, smoothing down her skirt. "I'll be ready for that sundae and a bite to eat when I return, if that suits you. I'm looking forward to our conversation." She turned that brilliant smile on him and sashayed through the doors of the hotel.

Now what was he going to do once he was left alone with his bride? Damn it! What could he possibly say to a woman who appeared as dignified as Miss Johnson? He knew from her letters that she'd worked as the head cook for the same large estate as Rose Granger. Miss Johnson's sophisticated manner took him by surprise.

Gabe Hawkins never had problems talking to the ladies before he'd sent for a wife. Why was this any different? Because it was just the two of them and Logan wasn't there to—to what? Guide a conversation between Gabe and Miss Johnson? Just because Miss Abigail Johnson was to become his wife didn't mean he couldn't talk to her normally. What kind of a life would they have if they couldn't communicate? A damn poor one, he figured. He wanted a wife he could talk to, laugh with, maybe even fall in love with over time.

Wife! Why the hell had he let the idea of retiring as a lawman possess him to send for a mail-order bride in the first place?

"So that's Gabe Hawkins," Abby mused with a song in her heart as she slipped out of the rumpled gray dress. "He is very pleasing to gaze upon. And he carries himself quite well with an air of quiet confidence becoming a lawman. Of course, he's not my Robert."

Sadness swept over Abby as she lay the dress across the only chair in the room. The thought of her late husband still panged deep in her heart even now. After all these years, the pain of his loss prickled deep in the recesses of her soul. The war was over; Robert hadn't come back. It would have put closure to the loss if she'd been able to bury him in the Johnson family plot. Instead, he lay under the ground somewhere in Manassas along with so many other souls.

Robert Johnson had no business going off to fight

in that damnable war. He'd had a wife at home and his elderly parents to look after. Instead he'd left that task to Abby, and when the time came to give them over to God, she'd been the one to handle their affairs, meager as they were. Robert had insisted a man of his education could be an asset to the war. He had reminded her that not every man who'd gone to take up arms could read and write. So he'd packed a satchel, saddled the old bay mare, and rode up to Camp Randall some thirty miles away. He trained as an officer then marched out to do his part. Remembering the painful past, Abby held back her tears. She'd not only lost Robert, but the family he'd promised they'd start as soon as he returned.

"Abigail Johnson! The dead are gone; best leave them buried after all these years." She swept away the threat of tears and inhaled deeply, resolving to do just that. It was past time for her to get on with her life, and Gabe Hawkins was the man to help her do so.

She laid out her maroon no-nonsense dress and began pulling the pins from her messy hair. Abby didn't like the weary look in her eyes, thinking it made her look older than her thirty-seven years. What must her soon-to-be husband think of his bedraggled mail-order bride? Gabe Hawkins looked so youthful with his sparkling blue eyes and dark unruly hair. He reminded Abby of a boy who'd just gotten away with something and could charm his way out of any sort of trouble. She smiled, thinking of the ways Gabe would probably use his charms on his new bride, thinking her none the wiser.

Abby slid into the warmth of the copper tub, her aching muscles relaxing. She smoothed the lavender soap she'd brought from home over her soot-embedded skin. Her mind gave way to the soothing scent and drifted off to a place of peace and youthful memories.

"Abigail Roberts, would you do me the honor of

becoming my wife?"

Robert was on one knee, beads of moisture dotting his forehead. Abby stifled the urge to giggle at the man she'd loved for several months. The self-assured man of her heart anything but confident as he knelt before her. Did Robert really think she'd turn him away after all these months of courting?

"I believe that I will, provided Papa has given his blessing." Abby's heart sang so loud she was sure the entire town could hear the music. She and Robert Johnson were finally going to get married, have a home and eventually a family of their own.

"I wouldn't have dreamed of asking you otherwise. Your father gave his blessing last week when I called on him." Robert stood, wrapping his arms around her.

She would always be safe there. Robert would make sure of it.

And he had...until the day he announced his intentions regarding the War Between the States.

"I am going to join the cause, Abby. I must do what I can to help those who need it most. We take our privileged life here for granted. While we have plenty, others suffer at the cost of long days in a cotton field with hardly any food on their table. Their daily lives begin before sunrise and end far after sunset. They live in constant fear. If I can help to change at least one person's life then I've done my part."

Their sweet and loving life together abruptly ended when Robert marched away from their happy life into a war that swallowed him whole.

"You have mourned long enough, Abigail." Robert stood in his tattered blue uniform, a stain covering the place where his heart was. "Be happy, my love. Find love again in this man; he'll take care of you." Then he blew her a kiss, turned and faded into the shadows.

"Miss Johnson?" A maid called out.

Her name, followed by a loud rap on the door, coaxed her out of her vision. The once warm water had turned cold and goose flesh trickled up her arms. Was she chilled from the cooled water or from Robert's visit? Since the end of the war Abby hadn't dreamed of her beloved deceased husband but a few times, each with an important message. The last dream had been when she'd sent Rose Duncan to Dodge City as a mail-order bride instead of going herself. Even in death, Robert was guiding her through dreams when it mattered most. This time was different. He'd never turned his back and walked away from her before.

"Yes, I'll be down in a few minutes," Abby called, climbing out of the tub.

Drying off, she hastily slipped into the dress she'd laid out then pinned a portion her hair back, allowing the fading dark waves to cascade over her shoulders. Glancing in the mirror, she smiled, feeling a bit like a schoolgirl. Robert had come to her in the dream. He'd told her to find love and to marry this man she'd been drawn to. It was what he wished for her…to find happiness and love in her heart once again. And so she would.

Abigail Johnson descended the steps to the lobby of Dodge House with the grace of a well-bred woman. Gabe's body flushed in unexpected need. For a woman a few years his senior, his bride was quite becoming. Her rich brown hair hung loose around her shoulders, accentuating her long, graceful neck. Deep coffee brown eyes reflected the schoolgirl lingering inside. She smiled and Gabe's heart exploded out of his chest and straight over to her.

"Miss Johnson, would you accompany me for a sundae?" Gabe offered his elbow, his nerves on fire at the thought this woman was soon to be his wife. All doubt of taking Abigail as his wife vanished from his mind. He'd never been surer he'd chosen the right woman. Would she feel the same when she learned once they were married he'd been transferred and would be taking her miles away to set her up in a house in Indian Territory?

"Mr. Hawkins." Abby placed her hand into the crux of his elbow, electricity jolting through him, "I do believe that would be the finest idea that has been presented to me since starting on my journey. However, you really must call me Abby if we are to be man and wife. Do you agree?"

Gabe nodded agreement as he guided her through the doors and onto the boardwalk. "Then you must call me Gabe."

"Gabe for Gabriel?" she asked keeping up with his long smooth stride.

"Yes. My parents named me Gabriel Samuel Hawkins after both of my grandfathers," Gabe said, remembering his grandfathers and the vastness of their plantations. Although both owned slaves, they abhorred the abusive practices by many of their peers and were disliked by many Southerners for their efforts in educating those in their care.

"It seems to fit you. Most lawmen can be perceived as heroes of God in the work they do to keep a town's people safe." Abby paused for moment, looking into Gabe's eyes. "I must confess, in my letters I didn't tell you that I wasn't born Abigail Johnson. Johnson is my late husband's family name. I was born Abigail Marie Roberts and have always been called Abby."

"You're a widow?" Gabe stumbled, raising his

9

eyebrows. *She isn't a pure woman? Does that mean— No! I will not allow my mind to take me where it doesn't belong—yet.*

"Robert went away to fight in the war. He lies with so many other lost souls at Manassas." Abby winced, her shoulders visibly drooping for a moment. "And what of you, Gabe? Did you fight in the war?"

"Yes, like many men did. I was in West Point when the war broke out." Gabe replayed that day when friends became enemies. When he was forced to choose which side he'd give his life for, right or wrong in the eyes of his family.

"Gabe!" Lilly Granger's little voice cried out running ahead of her parents. "Daddy said I could have ice cream with Momma's friend, Miss Johnson, after they get married today. He sent me over here to git you so's you can be his witness."

"Today?" Gabe cleared his throat, then rocked slightly back on his heels. He smiled wide, watching Lilly Granger scamper off with a skip and a jump. "Well, there really isn't any reason to wait now is there?"

Gabe guided Abby over to the Long Branch where a crowd was already gathering. It hadn't taken long for word of a wedding to reach the townsfolk. Together they gathered around Logan and Rose as Preacher Samuel began the ceremony. Gabe felt his vest for the folded piece of paper in the inside pocket. It wouldn't be long before he and Abby would be standing where Rose and Logan stood. They'd be saying their vows.

"I now pronounce you man and wife. Logan, you may kiss your bride." Preacher Samuel quietly closed his bible, and a swell of cheers soared up in the room when Logan swept Rose into his arms, claiming her with a kiss.

"Now it's our turn," Gabe whispered, taking Abby's hand in his. "Preacher Samuels, if you have the time to marry another man and woman, would you?"

"No," Abby whispered, trying to pull her hand from his. Gabe had a grip on it and he wasn't about to let go.

He looked down at her, his heart filled with desire. "We agreed to an arrangement. The preacher is here. The town is here. We've got witnesses. Why wait?"

Preacher Samuel smiled, opening his bible back to the place he'd just read from. "I believe I do, Marshal. Anyone in particular?"

"Yes, sir." Gabe placed Abby's hand in the crux of his elbow and brought her to the spot where Rose had just become a married woman. "Miss Abigail Johnson and I are to be married, this very day."

CHAPTER TWO

"Abby, I'm so happy you are here and that you've found someone!" Rose declared after the wedding, capturing Abby in a big hug that nearly squeezed the life out of her. "We never would have imagined Gabe, of all people, would take a bride. He's so lucky to have you. Now we'll be close to each other again."

"It was a bit sooner than I'd anticipated, but..." Heat radiated through Abby as she watched her husband standing in the midst of several prominent men from town, laughing and shaking hands with each of them.

Ed Masterson stood next to Gabe with a red-haired woman called Montana Sue. Mr. Collar had taken time from a busy morning at his dry goods store to give his congratulations to the happy couple as well. Even Mr. Hoover had attended, passing out several cigars from his latest shipment as soon as Preacher Samuels declared them man and wife.

There was a plain gold band on Abby's left ring finger that hadn't been there when she'd arrived in town. She should be furious; instead she was secretly grateful she hadn't had time to reconsider. When she'd started out this morning, she'd no intention of being married before dinnertime. She'd hoped at least to have an opportunity to become better acquainted with her husband-to-be before making it official.

Abby sighed, then smiled at Rose. What was done was done. *Sometimes fate just takes your hand and works its magic.*

"I guess that makes me Mrs. Gabriel Hawkins!" A surge of warmth suddenly traveled through Abby. She didn't need to turn around to know Gabe stood behind her as close as two strangers who'd just wed could be.

"I hope you're not too upset, Abigail. About not planning a wedding, I mean. I couldn't let the opportunity pass us by." Gabe's hand barely touched her lower back, yet the sizzle between them singed her skin clear through her dress.

Abby turned, feeling lighthearted as Gabe shifted back and forth. A shy smile peeked at the corners of his mouth. His blue eyes sparked with anticipation. Her heart responded like a drum, beating out a perfect rhythm.

"You did say there was no reason to wait." Abby slipped her arm into the crook of his elbow. The jolt of heat as he placed his hand on hers surprised Abby. It had been far too many years since she'd felt that sort of intensity within a matter of moments from a simple touch. The one and only time had been with Robert.

"So I did. Didn't see any reason for the good Preacher Samuels to have to come back when he was standing right there as if waiting for us," Gabe agreed, a hint of amusement in his words. "I do think it's time for me to get my new wife settled into our home, if you ladies don't mind saving your reunion for another day."

His gaze swept over Abby's face, and she felt her cheeks warm. For pity sake, she wasn't a young girl anymore, so why was she acting like one? Gabe Hawkins touched her soul in places she didn't even know existed.

"I will need to get my bags—" Abby bit her lower lip, the tingling in her fingers dancing with her twitching muscles. Why was she so nervous? She knew what being married was like. She knew what would be expected of her…or did she?

"No need, I sent word over to have everything you brought with you moved to the house. I suspect once word spread of our nuptials, preparations for your belongings were already being made. They'll be waiting for you," Gabe assured her, then tipped his head toward Rose. "Mrs. Granger, I trust we'll see you in a day or two."

"Yes, yes, of course," Rose stammered then leaned into Abby, her head inches from her. "If you need anything send word."

Abby nodded, matching Gabe's stride as they waded throughout the well-wishers. When they finally pushed through the swinging saloon doors, Dodge City seemed different to Abby somehow. She'd arrived an outsider, and maybe in many respects she would remain one for some time. But this was to be her home now. She'd make herself familiar with the people, sounds, and smells as time went by.

She thanked the strangers who'd gathered to share in their joy. When Montana Sue winked at Gabe, Abby couldn't help but wonder what secrets he held close to the vest. How much of their pasts would they share with each other? What else would be different now that she was married a man she only knew by the letters he'd sent?

Having only two to cook for rather than ten or more each meal.

Managing a small home rather than a large estate.

Not sleeping alone. Oh, goodness! It had been so long since she'd shared her bed. Did Gabe snore? Would he take all the blankets on a cold winter's night?

Would he want to claim her as the sun came up the way Robert had?

Abby swallowed, staring ahead. Robert hadn't placed any demands on her in their marriage. She ran the household as she saw fit, and Robert had been more than happy to have her do it. Would she one day say the same of Gabe? Her gaze swept from the rooftops to the fluffy clouds in the blue sky. *Please guide me with Your loving hand,* she prayed, her heart beating steady and calm. A feeling of belonging crept steadily through her. This was where she was meant to be. Gabe Hawkins was her connection to life again.

"Gabe, where is your—er, I mean, our home? I'm supposin' it's in town since you're the law here, but I hadn't taken notice of very many houses." Abby continued to scan up and down the street. As far as she could tell, the buildings in her sight were anything but proper places to raise a family or to start a marriage. Unless, of course, one owned a respectable business then lived upstairs. Even so, with the lack of children in town, she didn't think many families lived within the city limits.

"Yes, it is in town, just beyond the jail house." Gabe nodded across the street then patted her hand. "I must warn you. It's small compared to the northern homes you may be accustomed to, but I'd like to think it'll be comfortable for as long as we are in Dodge."

"'As long as we are in Dodge?' What has happened, Gabe?" Abby's heart raced as they made the short journey from the saloon to the single-story wooden structure. Surely if something important had come to pass since their last correspondence, her new husband would have at least mentioned it before they had married.

Gabe pushed open the door, avoiding her eyes. "I, well, I had put in my resignation. Instead it was rejected and I've been reassigned to Indian Territory. We leave by week's end."

It had only been a few days since the telegram from Territorial Judge Isaac Parker arrived, informing Gabe his services were needed elsewhere. And like it or not, which Gabe did not, Judge Parker was not a man to cross. Gabe's plans for an early retirement to devote his life to his wife and ranching up in smoke by the stroke of justice.

Gabe stepped over to the stove, checking the fullness of the pot of coffee, knowing full well it was cold as ice and a layer of sludge lay at the bottom. He needed something to do, anything to keep busy as he waited for the blow he was sure to come his way. Other than the good people of Dodge and his regiment in the war, he'd never had to account for his personal life before. Now he had a wife and, well, he wasn't sure how to handle that part of his personal life. As of an hour ago, he was now responsible for more than just himself. He had a wife, a beautiful woman who fired his heart and soul to care for.

"By week's end I'll be packing up again to move to an uncivilized area with a man I've just met and married, and you just now tell me?" Abby stood in the open doorway, hands on her hips with the sun blazing behind her. "How could you have forgotten something as important as being reassigned, Gabriel Hawkins?"

"I don't blame you for being angry, but what was I

to do, ride out along the railroad tracks and try to find you? I've got a fast horse in Spade, but not that fast." Gabe stoked the stove, then filled the pot with water, giving it a couple of swirls before dumping the morning coffee out the door. "I only got the news a few days ago, Abby. Judge Parker was clear in his orders. As soon as the new marshal arrives in Dodge City, I am to settle near a place called Fred, in Indian Territory. There is a man there who owns a trading post and a house that we can settle into."

She came up next to him, every bone in his body melting from the heat of her anger.

"Don't think for one moment the fact that there's a house waiting for us makes any difference!" Abby snatched the pot from his hands, then marched into the pantry. "It also doesn't make it any less serious that you didn't see fit to tell me our circumstances had changed *before* you took me as your wife!"

Gabe stifled the smile about to streak across his face. She was mad, and with good reason, but not mad enough to storm out the door and back to the Dodge House with her bags in tow. A good sign as far as he was concerned.

"If you'll be wanting a decent cup of coffee with your meals after tonight, Mr. Hawkins, you'll have to move the provisions to a lower shelf." Abby stretched to her full length, her fingers barely scraping the bottom of the top shelf, housing the coffee and other items she'd need for cooking and baking.

She was a fine woman indeed. Curvy and lean, full of fire and a spot of forgiveness as well. Gabe hoped those qualities transferred over to a passion he prayed lay beneath her proper surface. He couldn't wait for night to fall so he could explore those curves of hers fully.

"I'll do it first thing tomorrow, Abby." Gabe reached above her, heat scorching him as his chest pressed against her back. Everything in the world stopped. Everything except a pulse pounding blood through his veins. He inhaled the scent of lavender rising from her skin and hair. A calming and soothing fragrance, yet provocative to his unraveling senses.

Gabe wrapped his hand around the coffee can, pulled it from the shelf, and handed it down to Abby. She turned to him, her doe brown eyes wide and cautious. "Ah, what else do you need, Abby?"

"Cornmeal and any canned meat you have will do for tonight." Abby ducked under his arm, the can tucked securely to her chest.

Gabe gathered the cornmeal and several cans of meat, as well as some salt pork bacon and a loaf of bread he'd just purchased the day before. By the time he'd deposited the items on the table, Abby had already found the mixing bowls and baking pans. She opened the cornmeal, mixed in some milk and other ingredients Gabe purchased a few days before. Once she'd poured everything into a pan, she pushed it in the oven and set the table where Gabe stood watching in wonderment of her skills. He was definitely not going to starve.

Abby picked up one of her bags, dropping it on a chair. "Married less than a day and we are already on the verge of an argument. This is no way to start our life together, Gabe. Now, where is the bedroom? I'd like to unpack."

Gabe turned to her, his heart bleeding as he led her over to the room where they'd spend the dark hours of the night together with a wedge firmly planted between them. It was not how he'd pictured his first night as a married man. His first time married and he'd already sent his bride in a tizzy. And it was all his fault; he should have told her the moment he'd taken her over to the hotel. Only one thing to do—admit he was wrong and apologize.

"I'm sorry, Abby. I don't blame you one bit for being upset. If the roles were reversed, I would be also. And for the record, I don't like being moved to Indian Territory any more than you do. I had plans to retire and start ranching on a little plot of land just outside of town with my new wife. The last thing I wanted was to take my bride into wild and untamed country."

He strolled up behind her as she yanked item after item from the thread-worn bag. He gently trailed his hands over her arms and down to her hands. "I don't know how this works, Abby. I've never been married before so you'll have to help me out. Help me to understand what a husband should and should not do."

The tension in her shoulders eased. She turned in his embrace, gazing up at him, her jaw set and eyes alert. "As long as we are perfectly clear that I am not, under any circumstances, happy with this knowledge of moving to Indian Territory. There must never, and I mean never, be any secrets between us."

"My dear Mrs. Hawkins." Gabe put a hand in the air and covered his heart with the other. "I promise to always tell you as much as I can when I can as it pertains to our union." He allowed himself to hope that, for now, they'd have a peaceful night.

Abby tossed and turned while Gabe snored loudly from his makeshift bed on the front room floor in front of the fireplace. She'd hated to do it, but had sent him away from their marriage bed. And he'd gone, head hanging and a chuckle on his lips. It was a message she prayed Gabe would heed for the future if they were to have any sort of a comfortable life together.

The man was unaware the implications of deceiving a wife were different than tricking a woman here and there. Abby didn't want the first night of their marriage to be like this. One where they'd sleep apart, like strangers. Never mind the fact they were indeed strangers. She wanted what she and Robert had had before the war ripped him from her. She wanted Robert's gentle manner and consideration for her feelings, not Gabe's Wild West antics of what he presumed appropriate behavior with a wife. She wasn't some naive girl who'd accept anything a man told her, not that she thought Gabe was the type to purposely lead a wife astray.

She was Gabe's wife.

And Gabe was her husband.

Why hadn't he told her about the reassignment when she'd arrived on the train? Now that she looked back over the day's events, there'd been little time for him to tell her. No matter, he should have made an effort. Was he afraid she'd take the next train back to Wisconsin?

Would she have? She stared at the dark ceiling for a moment. No, she wouldn't have. But she wouldn't have married him right away either. She'd have stayed with Rose until she found a place of her own. Maybe she'd have given Gabe a chance to win her over with his blue eyes full of promise and love, and that mischievous smile of his promising a life, full and rich. Abby sighed, then punched the feather pillow into fluffiness.

Men! Such annoying sorts of mankind. She laid her head down, the gray of the night turning to shades of yellow and orange as the sun peeked through the window. A new day. A new beginning.

A day of forgiveness.

Coffee, rich with aroma, wafted teasingly around Abby. She laced up her boots, patted her hair into place, and stepped into the front room of her home. Her breath hitched in her lungs.

A shirtless Gabe stood at the stove flipping eggs and bacon, humming a tune she was unfamiliar with. Warmth trickled over her as she stood gazing at him. He was lean and well-muscled, perfection when he turned and smiled at her in a natural way.

"Good morning, Mrs. Hawkins."

Abby cleared her throat, smoothing down the front of her simple brown skirt. "I, ah, trust you slept well last night?"

"As a matter of fact, I did, considering it was on the floor and not in my own bed." Gabe chuckled, sliding the sizzling breakfast onto plates. "I have slept in worse places, and I thank you for not sending me out to the barn for the night."

A rush of regret spurred Abby's conscience as she slid onto a chair. "I'm sorry, Gabe. I was surprised by your announcement and—"

"You did what any wife would do. I understand that now, having had all night to think about it."

Gabe tugged on a blue cotton shirt, buttoning it slow and deliberate. Abby swallowed and put a fork full of eggs into her mouth.

"I made you a promise last night that I plan to keep. You'll never have cause to put me on the floor again, I can guarantee it."

Abby smiled at Gabe as he sat across the table from her, shirt well intact. The light reflected across his face and for the first time she noticed the bags under his eyes. *Slept well, indeed!*

"All right, Gabe. How much time do I have to pack up our home?"

"You mean you plan to remain my wife, even after you thought I'd deceived you?"

Abby laughed aloud. "Gabe Hawkins, you have a lot to learn about being married. Believe me, this will not be the first time we don't agree, but it doesn't mean I wouldn't remain your wife because of it."

"Word came that the new marshal is two to three days' ride from here. I'll arrange for a team of mules and a wagon for us." Gabe reached over, his hand covering hers. That sizzle of heat singed her again, sparking a surge of pleasure.

"Then I shall start immediately. First I must let Rose know my—*our*—circumstances have changed." Abby gathered the breakfast dishes and gazed at her husband as he walked from the safety of their home out into a town portrayed as having a wild reputation.

CHAPTER THREE

One week later

"Why did I give Abby the freedom to pack the household without my say so?" Gabe grumbled, placing the last trunk of the household items into the back of the covered prairie wagon then slamming the tailgate shut. Over the past few days while Abby had been making the preparations to travel to their new home, he'd been briefing the new marshal, Dale Rogers, on Dodge City and its people. He also gave him the lowdown on the trail bosses, drovers, and gamblers who came to town on a regular basis.

Dale Rogers seemed to be capable of the task and with Judge Parker's opinion that Rogers was his man, there wasn't anything Gabe could do about it. All the same, Gabe would feel a whole heap better when Marshal Jones was back in town from Missouri to run things.

It had taken some careful thought on his part, but Gabe had also mended a bridge or two with Abby, and for the past three nights had slept beside his wife. It hadn't been an easy task since Gabe had not only uprooted her life twice in the past few months but had also forgotten to tell her about being reassigned. Forgotten? Conveniently forgotten if he were truthful with himself, a mistake he'd not make again. Even now as he itched to get on the trail, he did not dare to interrupt her goodbyes.

"Everything will be fine, Rose. I'll write as soon as we arrive in, well, wherever it is." Abby swept a tear from her cheek then hugged her friend.

Gabe's heart pounded radically in his chest. Was he doing the right thing in taking Abby away from the only folks she knew in the area? Not that he had much choice in the matter, or did he? He would have resigned right then and there from law enforcement like he'd planned without his plot of land if he hadn't had to give thought to Abby's welfare. No, it was bad enough he was dragging her into Indian Territory so soon after their wedding. Whether he admitted it or not, being reassigned by Parker was better than the alternative of no roof over their heads or a lack of food on the table for a month or so. Sure, he would have found something eventually, but would Abby have stayed by his side? Would she have followed him further into uncertainty? Maybe. Maybe not. He'd bet Doc Holiday himself she would, that's how sure he was of Abby.

He smiled, watching his wife say her tearful goodbyes. Abigail Hawkins was a strong woman in heart, soul, and opinion. Gabe wouldn't have had it any other way, and he was proud she was his to grow old with. He didn't think it possible to lose his heart in so short a time, but he had. Abby was meant to be his and he was meant to be hers. Nothing was going to change that.

"You just got here and now you're leavin'. It ain't

fair, is all!" Rose whined, sniffing her nose loudly.

"It isn't, that much is true. Neither is life sometimes. It's all what you make of the lemons it gives you, remember that, Rose." Abby smiled, then turned toward Gabe, the smile on her face tentative at best. "Turn something sour into a pleasing taste and life will be all the sweeter for it, I promise."

"Those two are gonna weep like babies for days on end."

Startled by the sound of Logan's voice, Gabe reached for his gun.

"Hold on there! You're jumpy as a bullfrog in a pond." Logan stepped back, his hands in the air, far from the gun belt on his hips.

Shaking his head, Gabe holstered his firearm. "Sorry Logan, you startled me. Guess I was thinking deeply about those two."

"Now be honest, you were thinking about all those days and nights being alone with Abby with nothing but an occasional coyote call or prairie dog. I know I would be if it were Rose and me going in your place."

"I was wondering whether this wagon will make it in one piece or not. Abby has everything but the lumber from the house packed under this canvas." Gabe strolled around the wagon bed, checking each iron wheel for wear, the axles for any cracks, as well as the hound and tongue. He'd even inspected the grease bucket for a third time, knowing full well it was plumb full and there was plenty extra in the wagon bed.

"I'm thankful we're not traveling west over the mountains; we'd never make it without leaving half the cargo behind on the trail." Gabe chuckled, finally satisfied with the wagon and mule team he'd spent close to a fortune on. Spade, tied to the back of the wagon, whinnied, as anxious as Gabe to set out.

Logan placed a large basket covered with a red handkerchief into the jockey box. "Rose wanted to make sure you had some hardtack, sweetbreads, and preserves along the way. She's been putting them up for days now."

"Abby and I are appreciative." Gabe nodded his thanks, taking Logan's hand in his. "It's been a pleasure working alongside you, Logan. Take care of my town for me until Marshal Jones returns. That new marshal seems green to me."

"A Pinkerton always gets his man." Logan smiled, squeezing Gabe's hand a bit tighter.

"Abby, we really must be going," Gabe called out, checking the series of knots holding the canvas down over the bed of the wagon one last time.

Abby gave Rose a final hug then approached the wagon, her nose red and eyes moist from crying. Gabe placed his hands around her waist. Over the past few days he'd come to know every inch of his wife and his body reacted as he easily lifted her into the box.

"Bye, Rose. Give Lilly a hug for me," Abby said, dabbing her eyes with a handkerchief.

Gabe climbed aboard, rocking the wagon slightly.

"You take care of Abby, Gabe Hawkins, if it's the last thing you do!"

With a swift snap of the reins, the mules stepped out and the wagon lurched forward. Rose's words drifted away in the breeze as Gabe turned the team and headed south out of Dodge City.

***

"How much longer will it take to get to our new home, Gabe?" They'd been on the trail nearly a couple of weeks, the sun blazing down day after day. Abby tugged at the frayed ribbons of her bonnet, pulling the covering from her head. Her hair fell loose around her shoulders, and the warm breeze swept the heated beads of moisture from her neck. Even a hot breeze felt good to her in the unyielding heat since they'd set out this morning.

It was long past the urge she'd had to lean around in her seat to look back at Rose as they drove out of Dodge City. She'd lost her nerve about asking Gabe to turn back. She didn't think her husband, while he may have obliged her, would have appreciated it. Now she was thinking she should have; then she'd at least be on solid ground with a good bed to sleep in and a hot bath when she wanted it. Not one to complain, Abby had had her fill of the bumpy wagon, sleeping in the wagon on packed wooden crates or under the wagon if the ground wasn't rocky, and traveling in the endless heat.

At least she'd been able to bathe in a stream when they happened upon one. Never really a proper cleaning, she washed some of the trail dust from hair and body as quickly as she could. That was something and better than not being able to bathe at all. They'd had to sleep under the wagon only once since they'd set out when the heat of the night was intense. There was little room under the cover of the wagon for them both, but she'd arranged the crates and blankets in a manner that wasn't totally uncomfortable. It was better than sleeping on rocks while God knew what crawled around. She'd certainly gotten to know Gabe a bit more. Abby had slept wrapped in his arms safe and warm each night. Not an unpleasant situation.

"About three or four more days if the weather holds up and this wagon stays together. Might get lucky and arrive a day sooner." Gabe glanced over at her for a moment keeping the team lumbering forward. "I know it's been slow going and not so comfortable for you, Abby. I'm unfamiliar with this territory so there may be more places where we'll have to be on foot while I guide the team along. And if the next river we're to cross is high we may have to swim next to the wagon and hope it stays afloat, unlike the Cimarron which was low enough for us to drive right over and through."

"I'm not afraid of a little water, Gabe. Nor will I be opposed to getting off this hard seat and feeling the blood flowing through my veins again." Abby adjusted herself, giving emphasis to her words. She didn't think she'd ever feel anything on her backside again after the endless days of being jostled about. "It must be just as difficult and tiring driving the wagon as it is for me sitting here bouncing along at the will of the trail. I can't imagine what it would be like to control two bullheaded mules."

Abby swept some of the layers of trail dust from her skirt, then glanced over at Gabe as the wagon bounced over the rutted trail. The reins were loose between his long fingers and his strong hands hung relaxed. She'd no idea how he managed to guide the mules with so much ease. His hands and fingers were powerful enough to control two stubborn beasts pulling a wagon with all their worldly belongings inside, yet gentle when they skimmed across her skin at night. Her body recalled the ghost of his touch and she shivered with heat the memory left upon her.

"It depends. A light hand keeps them calm as long as you remember you are the one in control." Gabe gathered the reins in one hand then reached for her as if reading her spirited thoughts. Awareness sparked between them when his hand touched hers. "If you want to give it a try, I'll show you."

Abby quickly moved her hand from under his, rubbing the spot the spark bore into her. "No, not now. Maybe later on, just not right now. I feel guilty I've been of little help to you when we've stopped for the night."

The closeness of their persons next to each other distracted Abby. She had to keep her mind from wandering back to the nights after their departure so many days ago. The warmth of Gabe lying next to her. The tenderness of his kisses. The way her heart raced like a runaway horse even now.

"Abby, you've done more than you give yourself credit for. You've cooked our meals over an open fire, which I know you've never done before. You keep the wagon organized and clean, giving us a place to sleep in comfort rather than on rocky ground. Believe me, half of everything would be scattered through the wagon and I'd have used my saddle for a pillow rather than your soft breasts if left on my own."

Abby looked to the clear blue sky, shielding her eyes from the sun beating down on them. Her stomach lurched, and she knew it was well past time to eat. Or was it the thought of Gabe's head upon her? "Gabe, will we be stopping soon? I think we should at least get our feet on solid ground and have lunch, don't you?"

Gabe looked around, then turned the team toward a grove of trees. "Might be a good idea to give the mules a chance to rest. Getting out of the sun and a dip in the pond over yonder to cool off would be nice."

"A pond? Will I have time to bathe?" Abby couldn't keep back the giddiness she felt. "I do hope it's in a proper place, away from unseen eyes. It's been days since I felt clean, and I'd like nothing more than to really scrub the dirt from under my skin and nails."

Gabe laughed. "That's my intention. Keep in mind bathing with your husband could be a dangerous proposition, Mrs. Hawkins."

Abby felt a rush of heat that slowly settled on her cheeks. "Mr. Hawkins, you are quite a scoundrel!"

They'd lingered longer than he'd planned after bathing and having a quick bite to eat from the remaining preserves and bread in the basket the Grangers had given them. Gabe had found plenty of dry sagebrush for their fire and it burned hot. The prairie hen he'd killed and plucked waited for Abby to do what she would with it as their last meal of the day. The plucking task and gathering of more kindling for the fast-approaching evening kept his mind off of Abby humming *Golden Slippers*, a tune he'd long forgotten. When she quieted, Gabe had looked in on her to find she was propped against a bow of the wagon, fast asleep. Abby deserved a good rest at least once during their move into Indian Territory. He didn't have the heart to wake her, only to watch the gentle rise and fall of her breasts.

His wife continued to be a marvel to him. Abby rationed out their food, making sure they had enough for each meal but no more. Not once had she complained. Gabe couldn't have found a better woman than Abigail Johnson Granger. No sir, she was priceless and he'd do all he could to hold up his part of their marriage...to love, protect, and cherish. Ha, he'd even obey her if she asked him.

"Gabe?" Abby all but cried out from the safety of the wagon.

"Out here, Abby." Gabe smiled at the slight fear that edged her voice. Had she come to depend on him out of necessity, or was it something else?

She popped her head out of the back of the wagon, squinting at the sun setting in the west. "What time is it? You shouldn't have let me sleep, Gabe. Aren't they expecting you in a day or two?"

Gabe rose from his perch next to the fire. He

reached up, his hands circling her small waist, and lifted her down. "They can wait a day more. I'd much rather have my bride rested for the rest of the journey."

Gabe pushed away the lock of hair that fell across her eye and smiled at the pink that blushed across her cheeks. "Do you know how beautiful you are, Abby?"

"Gabe Hawkins, there are more important things than you losing your head over a pretty face. Is that dinner waiting for me to roast?"

Abby fluttered her lashes and he couldn't help but laugh at her. "Yes, it's ready and so is the fire. Tell me what else you need out of the wagon and I'll get it for you."

"I put some apples in water last night to soak; you can get those for me. We'll have some dried apple pie for dessert, and what's left of the hardtack Rose made." Abby picked up the hen, inspecting it thoroughly. "Salt and pepper, sugar, my spice jars, and a square pan as well. It should be in that box under the seat, along with a bit of bacon grease."

Gabe gathered up everything she asked for, setting them down on a crate before jumping down from the wagon. "Are you sure this is all that you need, Abby?"

He was amazed by Abby's skills in butchering a hen, even a prairie hen. She had the bird pieced out and in the pan before he placed the items she'd requested next to her. "That looks like it would feed a family of four rather than just two of us."

Taking the salt and pepper from the pan for the apples, she smiled as she seasoned the poultry. "That is why I do the cooking and you do, well, whatever it is you do."

"Humph, whatever it is I do. Nothing much but drive a two-thousand-pound wagon over a rutted trail and through riverbanks. Find meat when I can and prepare it for you to cook." Gabe stood next to the wagon, cleaning his knife. "I know I don't do much, but at least it's something."

"That it is," Abby commented continuing with preparing their dinner.

It wasn't long after the hen was on the fire that they were eating. The apple pie cooking over what was left of the fire smelled mouthwatering and Gabe couldn't wait to taste it.

"Abby, I don't know if I could possibly put another bit of food into my belly." Gabe sat back against the tongue of the wagon, stripping the last thighbone of its meat. He gave a contented sigh. The mules were grazing nearby and the sun had finally set in the west. He loved this time of the day on the trail with his wife.

"Then I'll leave the pie for the natives. I'm sure they'd love to have your leftovers, Mr. Hawkins."

"Mrs. Hawkins, if you do that you'll be walkin' the rest of the way. I ain't leaving no apple pie behind for the coyotes to feast upon, no sir."

Abby offered him a large piece. He took her wrist, pulling her down next to him. "I think we should share this one piece and save the rest for another day."

They sat next to each other, sharing the pie, the moon overhead bright in the clear night sky. Gabe wrapped his arms around Abby, pulling her closer to him. The fresh scent of lavender lingered in her hair from her earlier bath in the pond. He smoothed down a few stray strands then lifted her chin, capturing her mouth with his. He'd never wanted a woman in his life as much as he wanted this one.

Abigail ignited something in his soul he didn't know was there. A burning need to protect her. To serve her. To love her.

And he would do all three of those things for now

and for eternity.

CHAPTER FOUR

"Gabe! Look!" Abby pointed to the east at the cloud of dust rising over the horizon. "What is it from? Is there a cyclone?" Fear of being swept into a swirling devil chilled her to the bone. She wasn't ready to leave her new life behind.

Gabe pulled up the mules, shielding his eyes from the late morning sun. "Looks to be cattle on the move. A large herd, judging from the size of that dust cloud. Probably smell water up ahead. We'd best keep moving and stay out of their way." Except for the occasional Indian signs indicating a tribe was in the area, the dust kicked up by the cattle was the first real sign of life they'd seen since breaking camp.

"Oh, must we? I'd love to see them," Abby chirped, relief flooding her that the possibility of death wasn't imminent. Rising from her seat, she felt giddy as a girl on Christmas morning hoping there was a great gift waiting for her. She'd never seen Texas cattle before, or the men who drove them to market. It was part of the west she'd hoped to experience at least once in her life. *You are being so city right now, girl*, she laughed to herself.

"Sit yourself down and no, we are not stopping to watch them. I've seen a herd overturn wagons and trample horses and cowpokes. I don't plan on meeting my maker any time soon so get the thought out of your head." Gabe gathered the reins and urged the team of mules to move out. "As long as we stay west of the herd, we should be safe."

Abby watched the cloud as it intensified and then all but disappeared. Two riders came over the ridge, one riding toward them while the other turned back and out of sight. "Gabe, I think we've got company."

Gabe glanced around her, then pulled up the team of mules once again. "Looks to be a couple of cowpokes, chasing a longhorn most likely. Abby, listen to me, and get in the back of the wagon. I'll handle this."

"Are you telling me—" Abby struggled to curb her anger. It was rare for Gabe to treat her like a child, telling her what to do, and she didn't like it. "You'll not tell me what to do. We are partners in this marriage. No one rules over the other."

"You are my wife Abby. For now I'm telling you to get in the back of the wagon." Gabe tied off the mules, then checked his gun holster. "As your husband, it is my duty to protect you…always. So do yourself a favor and get your pretty little self out of sight."

"Well, I never!" Abby huffed, her skirt hiked above her ankles she crawled into the back of the wagon. She'd go, but only because if Gabe was getting his gun ready it had to be serious. Even so, she wasn't about to let him think he'd won—even if he had.

"No doubt, but for now keep quiet, Mrs. Hawkins," Gabe warned, a scowl deepening his brow. "And don't go peeking your head out to see what's going on either!"

Abby settled herself on a crate they'd shared the

night before cradled in each other's arms and her heart softened. He did a wonderful job in making her feel save—even loved a small bit.

Gabe drew the strings on the canvas until she was shut in. Her pulse pounded in time with the thunder of horses' hooves drawing closer. She bowed her head. *Please Lord, please keep Gabe safe no matter how insufferable he is at times. I trust You to guide him.*

"Howdy," Gabe greeted, his voice tense.

"Saw you as we chased down a stray. You coming from Dodge City?"

"Yes, on my way to the trading post in Fred."

"I've got about five hundred head I'm takin' up to the stockyard. Need to meet up with a Logan Granger about some cattle rustlers that have been hitting my herds the last few drives north."

"Logan Granger, the bartender at the Dodge House?"

"Unless there's two of 'em, the one I'm lookin' for works at The Lady Gay."

Muted light filled the wagon, spilling over Abby. She peeked out through the canvas. A man with whiskey-colored eyes sat on a big cream-colored horse. The man tipped his hat, reins in one hand and the other on the horn of his saddle. His smile was big, broad, and friendly. His eyes sparkled with surprise as she edged her way out in the open. He looked as much at home in the saddle as she did in the kitchen.

"Ma'am." His voice was deep and accented with a drawl foreign to her northern ears.

"Abby, darling. Come on out here and meet Cyrus Kennedy." Gabe gave her a hand, as she struggled into the jockey box. "If all accounts I'm familiar with are true."

"Now how would a homesteader know of Cyrus

Kennedy?"

"Marshal Gabe Hawkins at your service, Mr. Kennedy. I've been reassigned from Dodge City. Detective Granger and I were working on finding those rustlers. There are a few of your head waitin' for you at the stockyard," Gabe stated, helping Abby settle back onto her seat then he pulled her close. "Abby, this is Cyrus Kennedy, one of, if not the, richest cowmen in Texas. Mr. Kennedy, this here is my new bride, Abigail. Her friend just married Granger a month or two back."

"Ma'am, I truly hope you can keep this law-dog in line." Cyrus nodded, then pulled his hat off, shaking his head. "Whoosh, things have changed since I last had a correspondence from Detective Granger. Although we've not met until today, this one's a good man, judging from the way he and Granger have been handlin' those cattle rustlers."

"I have been doing my best, Mr. Kennedy, but he's an old dog and has yet to master a few commands." Abby joked, her voice light and airy, maybe a bit too airy for her own liking. She'd never earn Gabe's respect if she sounded like an empty-headed schoolgirl. Or worse, a domineering old woman.

"I have no doubt you have a handle on that task. You're the only one who's been able to tie him down." Cyrus laughed, pulling his hat down on his head. "We're looking to father the herd soon. Is there a place up ahead where we might do that?"

"About two hours up the trail is a grove with plenty of shade and grass. There's a river low enough to cross but plenty of water for the herd." Gabe took up the reins, adjusting them in his hands.

"Thanks, Hawkins. Ma'am, it's been a pleasure. That trading post you are heading for is up ahead. You'll be out of that wagon in a few hours." Cyrus Kennedy turned then spurred his horse toward the dust cloud rising again in the east.

"Now that was interesting!" Abby exclaimed, settling back onto the seat as the team lurched the wagon ahead.

Gabe eased slow and steady along the stage road leading to Fred. "We're almost there, Abby."

He was in no hurry to hand over his privacy with Abby yet. The first several weeks being married made him realize how much he'd needed a woman in his life. How much he actually needed Abby to keep him honest with himself. No woman had ever been able to do that.

"Thank goodness! I have grown tired of this jostling about. I'm afraid I may have permanent bruising on my—" Abby stopped short, and Gabe laughed out loud.

"Believe me, you do not have permanent damage on any part of your body." Gabe glanced over, smiling at the rush of color spreading on his wife's cheeks. After three weeks on the trail, their intimacies, he'd wondered at how she still blushed like a young woman. Abby was a widow, not unaware of the goings on between a man and his wife. Yet she acted like a young bride new to the ways of marriage.

Gabe found he loved that part of her beyond belief.

"You are truly insufferable!" She kidded, adjusting her sweet little bottom on the wooden bench. "These past weeks I have found how much I enjoy that side of you. You keep me on guard, sir. Don't change. Ever!"

"I will do my best to abide by your wishes." Gabe winked at Abby and reined in the mules. The need to hold her overwhelmed his senses.

"Is something wrong, Gabe? Why are we stopping?" Abby looked around them, her eyes full of questions.

Gabe jumped from the wagon then extended a hand. "There will be if you don't get down from there."

His blood burned like wildfire through his veins as her hand slipped perfectly into his. Her light girlish laughter filled his heart as she fell into his arms. Gabe gazed into her eyes, falling deeper under their spell. He held her against him to ease the pain of needing her next to him. He pushed a stray lock of hair from her face then covered her mouth with his, completely devouring her. He groaned as his body reacted to her melting against him. This may truly be one of the last uninterrupted private moments they'd have for a while once he took up as marshal in Fred.

"I couldn't wait for nightfall, Abby." Gabe kept her close, her heart pounding against him. "Once we get to Fred, we won't have much time alone with each other. You'll have the homestead to make feel like home. I'll have to see Colonel Frank Fred. I'll need to get word to Deputy U.S. Marshal Reeves and present my official papers to him, although I'm sure Judge Parker has already made him aware of my arrival. There's much to be done once we arrive."

Abby gazed up at him, her doe eyes sparkling with the same need he felt. "I will be waiting when you are done, Gabe. The cold, empty house will be warm and inviting by the time you find your way home."

"I was wrong in not telling you about the move when you arrived in Dodge. There will be many more things that I will do wrong. Promise me that you'll never let those indiscretions drive you from me." Gabe held her hand in his, watching his finger trace the lines of her soft palm. "These past four weeks I have grown to love you, Abigail. You are as much a part of me as breathing the air."

He looked up into her eyes, surprised to see tears trailing down her cheeks. "What have I done?" He pulled her next to him, kissing the top of her head. "Please don't cry. I didn't mean to make you cry, Abby."

She laughed into his shirt, then looked at him. "You haven't done anything wrong, Gabe. You've said exactly what I needed to hear. What I've longed to hear so many nights lying in your arms. I have grown to love you as well, and after Robert's death I wouldn't allow myself to dream of loving another man again. You have given me that dream, Gabe Hawkins."

"You never did tell me the full story of what happened to your first husband." Gabe's heart broke when she looked away to a place he'd never understand. A place where the love of her mate was lost and would never return. A place he hoped he'd never see. "I hope you share that with me one day."

"As I said, he was in the battle at Manassas with the Union Army. The letter was sketchy at best. We were told the Confederate Army attacked and killed the entire camp. Even the men who didn't have any way to defend themselves perished." New tears fell down Abby's face. Gabe wrapped her in his arms. "The letter said they were defenseless. Robert was there only to dispatch news to Washington; he wasn't supposed to be out in the field where the fighting took place."

Gabe's heart pounded against his chest, and his blood turned ice cold. He was at that battle. He was part of the 5th Virginia Infantry that marched upon Henry Hill that day.

"I'm so sorry, Abby. I'm so sorry that I've caused you so much pain."

She looked at him, her beautiful face devoid of color. "What do you mean, Gabe? What could you possibly have to do with Robert's death?"

"I was part of a unit that fought on Henry Hill that day. There were men wearing similar uniforms on both sides of the lines. It was difficult to tell where the enemy stood that day. So much blood was shed." Gabe looked away, fearing she'd see the terror in his eyes.

The pain of seeing his parents become cold and unloving when he returned home without his brother had broken him. The vow he'd made to never put himself or the woman he loved into that same painful situation. It was the reason he turned to becoming a lawman; it was a way of keeping his promise to himself.

"You? You killed my Robert?" Abby stared at him, disbelief replacing the love of moments ago.

"No." Gabe ran his hands through his hair, hoping for a memory, but found none. "I don't know, Abby. There were a number of lives lost that day. Chaos ran rampant that day on the fields. The southern politicians were so sure the war would end in that battle. Seemed like everyone was there watching. I was dispatched to Henry Hill. I'd heard there was a Union field hospital nearby. Lives were taken on both sides. I'm not sure if Robert was one of them. How could I be when there was gunfire all around me? How was I to know your husband would be there? Tell me, Abby."

Abby raised her hand, and he didn't move as it hit his jaw hard. "I hate you, Gabriel Hawkins!"

Gabe reached out and grabbed her as she turned from him. He pulled her shaking body next to his. Her tears soaked a spot near his heart. Gabe all too well understood. He'd lost his only brother to that damnable war. He had to make her understand there was no way of knowing he'd one day marry the widow of a man he may or may not have killed in the line of duty.

"Lives changed, starting that day—many will never

41

be the same on both sides. I lost my brother. I lost friends I grew up with through the years of fighting." Gabe released Abby just enough to gaze into her tear-swollen eyes. "So you see, Abby. I understand what it feels like. To feel your heart break. To know your entire world is crumbling and there isn't a damn thing you can do about it."

Abby stepped away from him and climbed into the wagon. "That may be so, Gabe, but forgiveness is something you'll find hard to come by for some time."

Abby sat as far from Gabe as she could, making sure even their clothing didn't touch. If not for the barely tolerable heat, she'd have gone straight into the back of the wagon as far as she possible could. She knew she wasn't being fair to Gabe. It was her heart that wouldn't let her openly admit he really had no part in Robert's death. She'd never expected that after all these years she carried the grief as strong as she did. The intensity of the feeling had taken her by surprise.

Not only had the war taken her first husband before his time, now it managed to put a wedge between her and Gabe.

Sooner or later she'd have to talk to him, for her own sanity if not his. For now she'd leave the brick wall of silence between them standing. He'd have to start and break it down before she did.

Abby stole a sideways glance at Gabe. Hidden under the Stetson, his gaze appeared to be focused on the mules and the road ahead. His lips were flat and the expression on his face tight. His jaw, strong and angular, was set in stone. A vein popping from his neck pulsed every few seconds.

Just say it, Gabe. Say what is on your mind and

let's get it all out in the open. Abby clinched her churning stomach when they bounced over yet another hole in the trail. Her mouth felt like she'd eaten a mud pie; she needed a drink of water. The road in front of her began to pitch. Abby closed her eyes for moment, praying her mind would stop swirling.

Reaching out, she grabbed Gabe's arm. "Stop, please stop. I think I'm going to be sick, Gabe."

"Whoa." Gabe reined in the mules, jumped from the wagon, and lifted her out of the jockey box. The concern on his face when he looked at her shook her resolve. "Abby, what's wrong? You look gray and green all at the same time."

Her feet landed on the ground, and she tested their stability for a moment before slumping against him. "I just need to sit out of the sun for a bit. Can you get me some peppermint out of the provision box? It might help sooth my stomach."

Gabe scooped her up and then gently set her down on the ground against a wagon wheel on the east side of the wagon. The bit of shade felt a little cooler than sitting in the box of the wagon had been. At least the world had stopped shifting before her eyes.

Maybe she was only overheated. That was it, too much time in the heat.

She heard Gabe clamoring around in the wagon then felt it sway seconds before his boots came into sight. Abby looked up as he knelt in front of her, a canteen of water in one hand and two peppermint sticks in the other. "I know you didn't ask for it, but you probably need some water."

"Thank you, my mouth does feel a little dry." Abby took a swig from the canteen, then leaned her head against the wheel. "How much further do we have to go? I'm so tired."

"Not much further now." Gabe drew lines in the dirt with a twig, looked up at her then dropped the twig in the dirt. Hands clasped and brows drawn together, he cleared his throat. "Abby, I...damn it, woman, how can I make things better between us? I don't think I can take much more of us not speaking. I miss hearing your endless questions. I miss the sound of you humming a forgotten tune now and again."

"Give me time, Gabe, please. I need to ponder it over in my head and come to terms with Robert's death all over again." She popped the peppermint stick into her mouth then passed the water over to him. Sparks tingled through her when his hand briefly covered hers. "I know you don't understand. Neither do I frankly. I thought after all these years my broken heart had mended. That I'd come to terms with his death. I don't know why that part of me opened up again. It's as if my heart won't let go. I hope you can understand."

Gabe slid down beside her, placing his arm around her shoulders pulling her to him, protecting her from something but not knowing what. He held her next to him, smoothing her hair in the blowing wind. "I understand more than you think. My younger brother was killed at Antietam. My parents never forgave me for not protecting him. They didn't care that we weren't in the same unit. Hell, we weren't even in the same area. All they cared about was their oldest son didn't protect his baby brother. In their eyes, they lost two sons on the battlefield instead of only one. And I lost my entire family when I rode west."

Abby swiped at the tears sweeping over her cheek. "I'm sorry. For your parents. For you. For Robert. For all the families who lost loved ones. It still doesn't make the hurt go away. It still doesn't keep old wounds from reopening."

"No, it doesn't." Gabe kissed the top of her head, then rose. "I'm gonna check the wagon and mules before we move on. Think you'll be able to travel then?"

Abby nodded her head, "I think so. If not, I'll manage. Maybe I should lay down in the back the rest of the way."

"If that's what you want." Gabe walked away, the heel of his boots raising dust as he made his way to the mules.

CHAPTER FIVE

Fred, Indian Territory

"Whoa!" Gabe guided the team and wagon around the trading post, glancing up at the cracked wooden sign hanging above the door before the wagon came to a stop. Cook's General Store was written in faded red paint across the board. He twisted around and gazed into the back of the wagon. Abby stirred a bit from her nest on their bed of crates.

Relief flooded his being. She hadn't become ill.

He'd been worried about her since they'd set out after the brief rest. Abby had looked a bit splotchy and shaken when she asked him to stop. Her pretty little mouth didn't hold the smile he'd grown to love, and she hadn't really glanced at him in a favorable way. The ease that had grown between them seemed dangerously close to disappearing. The sparkle in her eye had been replaced by something else he couldn't define. Certainly the fact that he and Robert were on the same battlefield hadn't caused her distance from him. She really didn't believe he had a hand in his first husband's death, did she?

Don't be half-witted. She has more sense than that.

"We're here, Abby. I'll go find someone and report in." The team securely tied off, Gabe jumped down. The wagon rocked slightly; Abby was moving about.

Thank you, Lord. Gabe sighed with relief. He'd grown more and more worried about his wife since they'd had the heated discussion about the war and Robert's death. Abby didn't seem the type to take to getting the vapors, so when they'd stopped he'd begun to think the worst. Why was she looking ill? Had she contracted a deadly sickness? Where was the nearest doctor in these parts if she needed one?

Gabe stepped through the door of Cook's General Store, glancing quickly around the small space. There wasn't much compared to the fuller shelves of Collar's in Dodge City. Abby was going to have to make do with what was readily available and what fresh meat he could bring home from a hunt now and again. A man came out from behind a ragged cloth covering a doorway, wiping his hands with a dingy rag.

"Can I help you?"

"I'm looking for Colonel Fred. Is he here?" Gabe inspected the man from his worn boots to his scruffy face. The man's slicked back hair hung to his collar in greasy strands. He looked to be a bit older than Gabe by a few years, but the lines on his weathered face said he was much older. Gabe wondered when the man had last had a proper bath.

"No sir, Colonel Fred doesn't come this way much. I'm Walter Cook. My brother and I own this place. Can I be of assistance?"

"I was to report to the Colonel upon my arrival. He's been expecting me." Gabe walked slowly around the small room. Animal hides hung on the wall, with sacks of flour, sugar, and cornmeal lining the shelves. A few bolts of cloth, but nothing fancy. There wasn't much in the way of specialty provisions or do-dads like those found in Dodge City. Abby wasn't going to be overly pleased and Gabe knew it.

I hope Abby can make do, Gabe chuckled to himself. *She's pretty resourceful; don't forget it for a minute, Gabe, ol' man.*

"You must be the Dodge City lawman." Cook harrumphed, thumbs hitched in his belt. "The Colonel said you was comin'. Not sure why we need a tin star in these parts, but the Colonel would skin me alive if I didn't welcome you."

I've been wondering the same thing. A lot of nothing going on around here.

"Yes, sir, Marshal Hawkins." Gabe understood how Cook felt; he didn't want to be in this godforsaken country either. "Well, then, I was told of accommodations, so if you'd point me in the direction of my home I'd be much obliged. I'm anxious to get settled. My mules need a good rest after this journey."

"There's a three-room cabin just down the road on the right along the riverbank. It's not much and needs a woman's touch, so if you're in need we can find one to fix it up for ya." Cook gave him a wink and a toothy grin. "Been empty for nearly a year now. Tenderfoots trying to make it in these parts don't last long. There's a lean-to shed for yer mules out back of the place. Our place is the big house up the road a piece."

"No, thanks. I don't think my wife would take kindly to another woman setting up house for her. I'll go take my wagon on down there and come back as soon as I've got it unloaded. I'll need to send word to Judge Parker that I've arrived, as well as Bass Reeves." Gabe quickly scanned the shelves once more. "Where do you get your flour and fresh meat from?"

"I trade some with the Chickasaw. The Moncrief ranch is up on the hill, might work something out with him on beef," Walter said, suspicion settling in his tired eyes. "Otherwise it comes on the wagon like most places around here. Ain't had no complaints Marshal, if that's what yer thinkin'."

"Thank you, I'll be back." Gabe left and stood just outside the door on the hard dirt. *Abby is not going to like this one bit, and I can't say as I blame her. Hell, I don't like it.*

Abby sat waiting for him in the jockey box, hands folded in her lap and the color of her face a bit rosier.

"We've got a place waiting for us down the road by a big house near the river." Gabe pointed then hopped back on the wagon and took up the reins. "Sounds like the place is in need of a woman's touch. It can wait until you're feeling better though, Abby."

"Gabe?" Abby's voice was soft and hesitant, her breath raspy as she drew in deeply then gazed down the road.

"Don't worry, Abby, I'll get the wagon unloaded. Tell me where to put the crates for you to unpack them." Gabe whistled and the mules moved out along the rocky, rutted road. "This is a stage road, so it might get noisy now and again, but I think it'll be peaceful most of the time."

"Gabe, I'm sorry for what I said back there." She put a hand over his and the intensity of the fire shooting through him caught him off guard. The heat warmed him clear down to his toes.

He smiled at her, then tucked her close to him. "We'll talk about it later. There is a lot of work to be done before we can think about...things. I don't want you doing more than you can if you're not well. I'm not sure how close the nearest doctor is and I don't want to take any chances on you feeling ill again."

Gabe allowed the mules to lumber down the road, passing a small river running to the south. They came to a large log cabin, complete with a lopsided door hanging off-kilter and windows with tattered curtains hanging in them.

"Looks like we're home, Abby."

Abby really was sorry for blaming Gabe for Robert's death. She'd been unable to stop throwing the accusation at him or control the anger that came from the depths of darkness hidden in her. *What is wrong with me? I've never acted so emotional before, not even with Robert's death. Hold your head high, Abigail, and bury your grief once and for all.*

She was a long way from the three-story estate where she worked as head cook to end up in a barely standing log cabin in Indian Territory. The realization was a hard pill to swallow. Abby could blame Gabe for that as well, and in a way she may have. In truth, the fault really was hers and hers alone. She could have stayed in Dodge City, but...

She'd wanted an adventure. It seemed she'd found one.

"The curtains look a bit tattered, but they'll do, won't they Abby?"

Abby looked down into Gabe's eyes full of questions. He stood next to the wagon waiting for her, waiting to take her home. Wondering if she was as fragile as she felt. *I'm not a fragile butterfly! I'll prove that I'm a strong woman, Gabe.*

"I'm sure they'll be fine. Once we're settled I'll make some new ones." Abby put her hands on his shoulders, desire and need surging through her when his hands clasped her waist, lifting her from the wagon. Their eyes met when her feet touched the ground. She smiled, touching his cheek lightly. *Lord, please let the house become a home. A home filled with love and caring. A home filled with many joys and laughter. A place Gabe wants to come home to. A place we can grow old together in.*

"I think it's time we made this our home, Mr. Hawkins." Abby smiled then stepped out of his arms. Strolling across the porch to the door, a shiver ghosted down her spine. A warning of sorts? Pushing open the door, a breath hitched in her lungs.

"For the love of—" Abby stood in the main room which would serve as kitchen, dining, and living rooms. A stove stood lonely along the east wall near what she believed to be a sink, a single kettle on a burner sprouting plants from the seeds a critter had left behind. The floor, although rudely constructed of wooden planks, was quite dirty from clumps of dirt and leaves that had fallen through the cracks in the roof. *Nothing a good sweep of the broom and a little patching can't take care of until Gabe can put a proper roof on.*

The hearth was cold, but someone must have loved this house at one time. Split logs leaned against the walls near the fireplace for the next cold night. Abby ran a finger through the dirt on the mantle, visualizing the items she'd place there.

Abby strolled slowly toward the back of the kitchen into a small, narrow room near the stove. Filled with rows of shelves, the space would serve as a pantry once Gabe moved them down to where Abby could reach their provisions. There was plenty of room for what they had left from their journey. She would make a list for Gabe of what was needed and they'd soon be plumb full.

Holding her breath, Abby pushed through a half-opened door. She knew this was to be their bedroom, the place where she and Gabe would share each night, curled up in one another's arms. A bed made from logs and a rather ratty mattress stood along the back wall. The room had two windows, one facing the west and the other on the south wall. Tattered lace curtains hung over the graying windows. *Definitely a woman's home at one time. Gabe will be happy I insisted our bedroom furniture be brought in the wagon once he sees this bed.*

Abby stepped over to the room next to their bedroom. The door creaked on its hinges as she pushed it open and stepped in. Her hand flew to her heart as tears bordered her eyes. There had been love and laughter in this home at one time. She walked around the room half the size of the other bedroom. There was a small bed along the inside wall made of the same materials as the adult-sized one they'd replace. On the opposite wall sat a small crib, a threadbare blanket crumpled in one corner. Abby picked up the blanket and the moth-eaten rag doll hidden beneath it, hugging them to her chest.

Yes, this was the perfect place where she'd make their home. They would bring joy and laughter back to live within these walls once more.

A shadow passed over her and she smiled, the joy chasing away the despair threatening to creep over her.

"Lord, Abby. I had no idea it would be this awful. That I'd be taking you to something like this." Gabe's arms wrapped around her, dissolving any fears she may have had.

"It's perfect!" She turned, gazing into the worry dimming his otherwise brilliant blue eyes. "It's not so bad, Gabe. With only a few touch-ups and a good sweeping, it'll be right as rain. A home in no time at all."

Abby took his hand, leading him through the front room toward to door. "Come on now, let's get unloaded so I can get things settled while you go back to the post."

Abby hoped she sounded upbeat, unlike the twisting in her stomach warring with the joy in her heart. *It might take a month of Sundays to get this cleaned up, but it'll be our home forever.*

By the time Gabe placed the last crate in the house, Abby already had the floors swept, the pantry shelves cleaned, and the fireplace mantel wiped down. A few trinkets and pictures took up residence there, a small start in bringing the place to life.

"Would you mind fetching me a bucket of water from the river? I'd like to get these windows where I can actually see out them," Abby called out from the pantry where she'd been filling the lower shelves with the remainder of their Dodge City provisions.

"As long as you don't work yourself into exhaustion! Things don't need to be done in one day, Abby." Gabe headed out the door and down to the river with the one bucket they had in his hands.

The mules were already in the lean-to and the wagon was put up until needed. Spade chewed lazily on some grass under the shelter of a tree next to the shed. Gabe slipped down to the riverbank, scooping the bucket into the slow-moving current. The birds sang cheerfully from somewhere in the trees and the scurry of squirrels rustled in the brush. Sounds of nature he hadn't heard in many years.

Pulling the bucket up, Gabe thought of how peaceful it was here as he leisurely strolled back toward the house. *I may not miss Dodge after all if every day is like this one.* The air was fresh and clean. No one was trying to shoot the other for simply looking at someone the wrong way. The only music came from nature itself. Yes indeed, Gabe could get used to this way of life mighty quick.

The sound of hoofbeats brought his head up. A lone rider approached, the white horse under him as sleek as new-fallen snow on a winter's day. The man reined in at the front of the house, a rifle hung from the saddle.

"Howdy." The black man sat lazily in the saddle like he'd born to it. Easy and confident. His face was serious; cold, dark eyes taking in his surroundings in a quick sweep.

Gabe tipped his head, placing the bucket on the ground, never taking his eyes off the stranger. "Howdy. What can I do for you?"

"I'm looking for Marshal Hawkins. Heard he was to arrive from Dodge City today."

"Yes, sir, that's what I've heard." Gabe's hand dropped near his holster and slid the corner of his jacket behind a gun grip. *What kind of hell has landed at my doorstep?* "And who might you be, so if I run across the lawman I can say who is looking for him?"

The man moved the front of his vest aside, revealing the star of a deputy U.S. marshal. "Bass Reeves. Judge Parker sent me to make sure he'd arrived in one piece, and to introduce myself."

Gabe smiled, hoping his surprise, and suspicion, hadn't been too obvious. "Marshal Reeves, glad to make your acquaintance. Mrs. Hawkins and I arrived a few hours ago. Please, come inside. I'm not sure how much Abby has accomplished in the last few minutes, but you're welcome at our table just the same."

Bass dismounted, tying his horse to a post on the porch, then extended his hand to Gabe. "Marshal Hawkins, nice to meet you. And I could use a good cup of coffee, if there's one available."

Gabe shook the hand of the one man outlaws on the lam in these parts hated most. Gabe had never seen a picture of the infamous Bass Reeves, but he'd heard tales of his reputation in always getting his man and serving justice, including his own son. "No promises, Marshal, but Abby will come up with something."

Gabe and Bass strolled across the porch and into the house where Abby already had coffee and biscuits waiting on the table. Pride soared through Gabe; Abby never ceased to amaze him.

"Abby, this is Deputy U.S. Marshal Reeves." Gabe sidled up next to Abby, putting a protective arm around her waist. *Just making sure he knows she's mine and no one else's, not that he has any ideas on making it otherwise.* "Marshal Reeves, this here is my wife, Abby."

"Ma'am." Bass tipped his head, then placed his hat on the table in front of him, waiting to be invited to sit down.

"Marshal, I hope you don't mind plain ol' biscuits. I'm still settling things in the pantry." Abby smiled, motioning for Gabe and their guest to sit.

"No, ma'am. I'm used to hardtack so these biscuits are a welcome change. Thank you." Bass took his place at the table, his back to the pantry.

"Marshal, what can you tell me about this area? I haven't been given much information on my duties here. In Dodge, it was the usual task of keeping the gamblers honest, the gunfighters out of trouble, and the citizens safe." Gabe slid in to the chair at the end of the table where, like Reeves, he could see the door clearly.

"I don't mind if you call me Bass, if you are so inclined. May I call you Gabe? Or is Hawkins more fitting?" Bass dunked a biscuit into his cup, then popped it into his mouth.

Gabe laughed. "Either is fine, whichever rolls off your tongue easiest will do."

"These are mighty fine biscuits, ma'am. Reminds me of my wife's." Bass's smile reached from ear to ear as he ripped another biscuit in half and dunked it into his coffee mug. "It's pretty simple. I may need assistance from time to time when I've got a writ for an outlaw. It may be quieter than Dodge City, but no less dangerous. Here a man of the law never knows if there's a gun pointed at him from behind a bush or tree, or even an outhouse."

Gabe nodded his head, studying Reeves over the brim of his cup. Suddenly he realized Judge Parker may have had good reason to decline his resignation and reassign him to Indian Territory.

CHAPTER SIX

Several weeks later

Abby was putting up the last of their belongings when there was a soft rap at the door. She froze for a moment, unsure whether or not to answer. She'd not had the opportunity to meet anyone yet. Gabe had met the owner of the trading post where he'd gone to purchase the items of her list. Other than that, Gabe hadn't said to expect anyone, but then it seemed some people just showed up unannounced.

"Hello, is anyone home?" The soft lyrical voice filtered through the door. "Mrs. Hawkins, are you at home? I thought you might—"

Abby swung open the door and her heart melted, along with her suspicion. A woman of about Abby's age stood on the porch with a pot wrapped in some towels in her hands. The woman's smile was tentative at best, as if she were afraid to say anything.

Baked beans. Maple. Abby savored the sweet aroma followed by the saltiness of ham.

"Hello. Can I help you?" Abby smiled, happy to

discover the possibility that another woman lived near enough to bring over a hot, or at the very least, a warm pot filled with food. Abby looked up, breathing in deeply to ease the tension in her. *What to make for the supper meal resolved by the generosity of a total stranger. Thank you, Lord.*

"I'm Mrs. Walter Cook. We live in the house just down the road." Mrs. Cook turned, pot and towels in her hands, to the east than looked back again. Her bright eyes, matching the cornflower blue of her dress, sparkled. "It's been so long since another woman has been in this house. I hope you've been able to make it feel like home in so short a time. I know you just arrived."

"Yes, so far I have; but there's a long way to go yet, I'm afraid." Abby blocked the doorway, wiping her hands down the flour-sack apron.

"I'm afraid I'm a bit late on thinking you could use some home cookin' on one of your first nights in Fred. Walter advised me to give you plenty of time to adjust to your new home." Mrs. Cook offered up the pot, towels and all. "I'll come back another day, when you're settled in a bit more."

Suddenly realizing her bad manners, Abby stepped aside. "Oh, please forgive me. I don't know what's become of my manners." Abby took the offered pot, holding the door open with a hip. "Please do come in, Mrs. Cook."

Mrs. Cook's smile reached her eyes and Abby felt a surge of ease.

"My name is Matilda Cook. I do hope you'll consider calling me Millie."

Abby placed the warm pot on the stove, then turned toward her guest, folding the towels as she walked to the table.

"I'd like that, Millie, as long as you call me Abby. Abigail is such a mouth full." Abby chuckled, pouring two cups of warm coffee. "I've sent my husband to the trading post for a few things. I hope you don't mind the bottom of the pot coffee today."

"Heavens, no. I'd drink whiskey if it meant having someone other than Walter to talk to." Millie sipped her coffee like a woman born on the wealthy side of the street—dainty and slow. Abby wondered what could have brought such a refined lady to the middle of nowhere.

"Where are you from, Abby?"

Matilda Cook, regardless of her friendliness, was a stranger. Abby hesitated about how much to say regarding Gabe and herself.

"Of late, Dodge City by way of Wisconsin." Abby slid onto the chair across of Millie, then took a sip of the lukewarm coffee.

Millie nodded, setting her cup back on the table. "We came here from Kentucky a few years back. Walter and his brother decided to come out here and open a store. Well, a trading post really. What they call a store is far from what I did my shopping at back home. Anyway, they have grand ideas for a thriving business, thinking this wilderness will be populated with people from the east. Personally, I don't see it. All I've seen are men dragging their families here and then hightailing it back to where they came from." Millie tsked, gazing at Abby with a hopeful glint in her soft eyes. "Do you have any children?"

The one empty spot in Abby's heart pinched and warmed slightly. All resolve regarding Mrs. Matilda Cook vanished. "Gabe and I were just married a few months ago. Neither of us are expecting children so late in our lives. We have each other; it's all we need."

Millie's eyes bore so deep into Abby that she had to look away. She didn't want a stranger to see the desire she'd never have fulfilled. Did the sadness, the emptiness of being childless show in her eyes? Had her heart betrayed her and revealed the secret wish for something Abby would never have?

"Hmmm, well. I really must be going before little Charlie comes in from the store." Millie smiled, then pushed away from the table. "It's been real nice chatting for a minute with another woman. The family who lived here before left before the heat of summer rose. The place has been empty for over a year now. It needs a family to love it."

Abby walked her new friend to the door. Millie paused for a moment then shuffled across the porch.

"I do hope you'll come and visit soon. Once the cold weather sets in, the road can be dangerous. Sometimes ice and snow cover the path, making it treacherous." Millie reached out, pulling Abby so close she could feel the woman's breath on her cheek. "Be careful, Abby. You don't want to lose that little one before he gets to meet his papa."

Millie lighted down from the porch, then turned, giving Abby a bright, wide smile and wave of a hand as she strolled back down the road, humming a lullaby.

Abby stood, mouth gaped open, unable to respond. Mentally she ticked off the days since she'd last had her monthly. "No, it can't be" The world began to sway and she grabbed a post to steady herself. Joy and knowing spread its warmth clear through her heart straight to her tummy where a hand covered it protectively.

"A baby! We're having a baby!"

***

Gabe scanned over the list Abby had written for him. Spade lumbered along at a leisurely pace on the road leading to Cook's. It felt good—the peace and quiet. Soothing. Relaxing. Reflective.

"I hope they have all these things Abby says we need. How does she think I'm going to get a couple of sacks of flour and cornmeal home? And what are fancy plums anyway?"

He shoved the list back into a pocket and moved with Spade. Gabe wasn't in any hurry to be back home, and he didn't rightly know why. Abby's list of chores for him had grown the longer he hung around. She cast about orders as if she was running a big house rather than their ramshackle little cabin. He felt more like a servant than her husband until supper was served...and they'd retired to bed.

He'd held her in their bed for the first time in weeks. No rocking of the wagon in the wind. No critters scurrying under them. It was just the two of them, alone. Holding each other. Loving each other. Abby had a way that made him feel things he'd never felt before with any other woman. Even now his body reacted to the memory of the night. Damn but the woman was a marvel in so many ways.

The way Abby had the table ready for their unexpected guest the day of their arrival sent a surge of pride through him. And her reception of Bass Reeves sharing biscuits and coffee with them was a miracle. Why should he consider it a miracle? Abby was from the North where there weren't slaves working the fields or ushering people about in the big houses. She accepted people for who they were. Just one more thing for him to admit to in his admiration of his wife—Abby was everything he could have hoped for and more.

Abby had a good heart, a kind heart. A sense of respectability. A kindness he'd not felt since the War Between the States had begun. Before every man with a gun was regarded with suspicion. Before men, like himself, set out to tame the west. At least here in Indian Territory civilization was slow to put her boots on the ground. If only it would remain so.

Now if Cook's had what was on his list, he could go back home to Abby with a smile on his face and a grumble in his voice as to the toll the weight of the sacks of flour and cornmeal took on Spade's back. No sense in making her think he was happy to do her bidding, which of course he was.

Despite himself, a grin spread across Gabe's face and he chuckled. "Admit you love doing for her," he muttered, reining up to the hitching post in front of Cook's.

"Hey, Walter!" Gabe tied off Spade then slid the supply list from his pocket before walking into Cook's. "Abby's got a list a mile long here. I don't suppose you have 'fancy plums' by chance?"

Walter's throaty laugh was all the answer Gabe needed. "Not rightly, but reckon I can put in a request next time the wagon comes through. Course, not sure how good they'd be by the time they arrived."

"Hmmm. Well, let's do the best we can then." Gabe handed over the list then rocked back on his heels as Walter began gathering Abby's items. The store hadn't changed since they'd arrived a few days before. Why would it? No supply wagon had come through during the night. Only the sounds of night creatures outside their window and on their roof.

"Did Marshal Reeves come by?" Walter placed a slab of salt pork on the counter, then crossed the item off.

"A few days after we'd arrived. I nearly blew his head off, the man snuck up on me by the riverbed." Gabe laughed, remembering how he'd clamored for his sense of mind.

"He's good at that." Walter moved from shelf to shelf, gathering items in a neat pile. "I sent word as soon as I seen your wagon coming down the trail. Good thing he was in the area. Been huntin' down some members of the Jesse Evans gang."

"There a big problem down here with outlaws?" Gabe walked over to a window, peering out over the vast, empty land. Not a soul in sight.

"All I have is a one-pound sack of cornmeal." Walter put the sack on the counter then reached for another item. "Them outlaws make a trail between here and Mexico, thinkin' the long arm of the law don't come this far. But Marshal Reeves, he finds 'em and takes 'em in alive to be judged."

"That'll do until you get the next shipment in." Gabe turned from the window, running a hand through his hair. He thought of the streets of Dodge where a gunfight took place where everyone could see it. Out here, danger lurked behind every bush or down a river bend. "Could be why Parker sent me down here then; one more badge can't hurt."

"The cowpokes raise hell once in a while if they stop for a bit. There's been more cattle rustlin'."

Gabe grew nervous thinking of Abby alone in the cabin. "Is my wife safe at home?" he muttered to himself, taking a deep breath to calm the rush of anxiety threatening to take hold of his common sense.

"Millie's been up at our place with the youngin' most times alone. Once in a while I bring Charlie here if she's got it in her mind she needs peace. Like today, she had a pot of maple beans and ham cooking for y'all." Walter began figuring the bill for Gabe's purchases, then packed what he could into an old flour sack. "Do you have children, Hawkins?"

"No." Gabe's heart bottomed out; children were never a consideration. "In my line of work it's dangerous enough to take on a wife, but having children…"

Walter smiled, pride filling his eyes. "Children are an extension of you and your wife. They are the thread to keeping your legacy alive when you're gone. Charlie, come on out here and say howdy to Marshal Hawkins."

Gabe looked at the dark-haired boy of no more than seven or eight with eyes as blue as the sky who came out from behind the curtain. His smile was big as he walked over to Gabe and shook his hand.

"Marshal Hawkins, nice to meet you." Charlie stood straight, his hand tight around Gabe's.

"Charlie." Gabe nodded, his stomach flipping like a boulder down the side of a mountain. "I hope you come and meet Mrs. Hawkins; she'd be mighty happy to see you."

"Yes, sir," Charlie said then went back behind the curtain.

Walter picked up the flour sack filled with provisions, handing it over to Gabe. "As soon as a new shipment comes in I'll have more cornmeal."

"What do I owe you?" Gabe slung the sack over his shoulder then gathered the smaller one that held the meal and flour.

"Twenty-five dollars. You can settle up with me in a few days." Walter walked alongside Gabe.

Gabe tied the two sacks on either side of his saddlebag, then took up the reins in his hand. "See you in a few days then. Nice boy you've got there." Gabe rode away realizing that his perfect family was missing something…or someone.

***

Abby sat down on the stoop of the porch, the housework waiting for her inside forgotten. There were biscuits to be made to go along with the beans and ham warming on the stove. The pantry needed to be organized for the provisions Gabe had gone to the trading post for. The tattered curtains needed to be mended and washed.

The baby's room needed to be scrubbed and… She knew nothing of taking care of a baby. Abby could manage a large household of servants, but when it came to a baby, the thought of being responsible for a helpless human being scared the daylights out of her.

And worried her.

Would she be a good mother? A loving mother? What if she forgot to feed the child? What if the baby got sick? Who would care for it? Where was the nearest doctor? What if she lost her child and her heart?

"Oh goodness, I don't know how to give birth. What if I hurt my baby? Who will help me bring the little one into the world? Certainly not Gabe!" Millie's face perched itself in Abby's mind, a smile on her face. "Yes, of course, Millie will know what to do."

She drew in a breath of relief and watched the road leading to the trading post for Gabe to come back home. How was she going to tell him his new wife was carrying his child? A sweet, innocent baby neither of them gave a thought to creating when they'd lain with each other.

What if Gabe sent her away?

"Lord, thank you for this blessing." Abby laid a hand gently on her abdomen where a life grew inside. "Please guide Gabe into seeing our child as such—a blessing of love."

Looking down the road one last time, she rose, dusted her hands down the apron, then strolled back into the cabin. She drifted past the table where she'd had coffee with Millie not long ago. Past the fireplace and chairs where she and Gabe had eaten warm applesauce after a late supper last night. Past the door to the room where Gabe held her last night, loving her fully and completely.

Abby padded with hesitation into the next doorway, pausing after crossing the threshold where children had once slept. The room where her baby would sleep.

Gabe's baby.

Their baby.

Abby swiped at the tears threatening to burst from her eyes. She smiled then moved further into the empty room and made a trek around the parameter. "Well, little one, your mama has some work to do before you arrive. And your papa will build you a fine crib to sleep in."

"Crib?" Gabe's sudden question stabbed at her heart as she felt his hands settle on her shoulders, turning her until she faced him.

The fear in her heart gave way to something close to unconditional love. Something she'd not felt until that moment, looking in Gabe's eyes. Eyes filled with questions, not anger.

She smiled, nodding "Yes, a crib."

"When? How?" Gabe's face reflected the shock she'd felt when her pregnancy was realized.

Abby laughed. "As to the when, I'd say somewhere between Dodge City and here. As to the how..." Abby felt her cheeks warm, remembering the way Gabe made love to her. His hands skimming slowly over her, igniting her skin through and through.

Gabe gathered her into his arms, holding her close for a moment. She gazed up into his eyes where unbelievable, impossible truth quickly turned the seed of joy into a dying sprout. He let her go and a cold blanket enveloped her.

"How are we going to provide for a baby when come winter we may barely be able feed ourselves?

Abby we are out in the middle of nowhere. There is not a doctor around the corner. No way to get medicine if needed." Gabe paced the room then pushed past her and out the cabin door.

Abby's stomach took a tumble. Her hands quivered. Stinging tears of sadness welled up in her eyes as she fought to hold them back. She watched Gabe stomp back in, carrying the items from Cook's in his arms, then unceremoniously dumping the flour sacks onto the table.

Gabe pulled item after item out of the sacks. "This isn't half of what was on that list of yours." Gabe ran his hands through his hair, his face scrunched with concern. "How am I to feed my family when what is needed isn't readily available?"

"Have faith, Gabe. We'll survive out here as Millie and Walter Cook have. Our love and faith will guide us." Slowly, Abby reached out, her hand lightly touching his arm. When he shrugged away from her the sting of his rejection burned her heart. Abby bit back a whimper and took to sorting through the provisions scattered across the table, her mind reeling.

Give him a minute and then he'll come to terms with being a papa. He's in shock, nothing more. He's not going to reject...but what if he does? What if he doesn't want me or our baby? Nonsense! Pure nonsense.

Abby walked over to the stove, stirring the beans and ham for a few minutes. She listened as her husband wore a path across the floor from the table to the fireplace. Grabbing a bowl, she measured out the ingredients for the biscuit batter. She glanced up from her mixing when the pacing stopped. Gabe stood next to the fireplace, his broad shoulders slumped in defeat.

"Would it really be so bad? Having a child?" Her fingers working the dough, hope filled her heart.

"At our age?" Gabe pondered, hands against the

mantel of the fireplace. He shuffled his feet in the soot on the hearth from last night's fire. "We'll be too old to keep the boy out of trouble. And what would happen to the two of you if I was killed? Who will be here to provide and protect you both?"

So that's it! He's worried about his family. His little boy. His responsibility and pride. Abby smiled, spooning out the dough. "Well, that's something to think about when the time comes. And believe me, Gabriel Hawkins, I am not ready to give you up yet!"

"One day you may not have a choice. One day an outlaw may decide to shoot a marshal for no good reason."

Abby looked up at the sound of the front door closing, then watched as Gabe rode away.

CHAPTER SEVEN

Gabe rode hard and fast, giving Spade his head. He rode blindly, not knowing or caring where he was as long as it was away from talk of a baby. Specifically, the responsibility of a baby.

After the war, all he thought he'd wanted was a comfortable life alone. Then he witnessed what love could do for a man and took a risk by placing an advertisement for a wife. Abby came into his life like a new promise. He didn't want to leave a fatherless child behind, nor leave Abby as a widow. That wore on his heart more than anything. Now that she had firmly planted herself there, he'd do anything to protect her.

Instead he was on the verge of abandoning Abby and their unborn child. If he kept riding out, he'd be far from them. Far from feeling the pain of losing a child. A wife. Love. Family.

Was he really that man?

"Whoa." Gabe gently pulled on the leather in his hands. Reining Spade in, he noticed the white foam of sweat on the horse's neck for the first time. Sliding out of the saddle, he grabbed a canteen from a saddlebag and came up his horse's nose.

"Sorry, boy," he said, pouring water into a cupped hand, allowing Spade to slurp from it. "At least you got to stretch your legs out. And I got to be your behind."

When had he ever run from anything? Even when his parents told him to leave he hadn't, at least not right away. He'd tried everything from prayer to crying and begging at his father's feet to forgive him for not protecting his younger brother. Gabe stayed, hoping his parents would get past their grief until it became abundantly clear he was unwelcome and dead in their eyes...and hearts. They had no more love for him. Defeated, he'd ventured out west to tame its wildness as a lawman. To look death in the eye and dare it to take his life.

But Abby is different. Abby had nothing but love in her eyes. In her heart. And it was all for him...and their unborn child. Why was he running away when he should be running into her arms, smothering her with kisses? Hold her tight, as if his life depended on it.

Gabe brushed the crust from his horse's coat where the heat of the evening breeze had begun to dry the sweat. On the western horizon, the bright orange sun sat in the sky in hues of red and pink. A time for reflection of his fears, of really giving his heart without question.

You're a damn fool, Hawkins! You left your pregnant wife because you don't want to deal with the possibility of heartache. Abby doesn't deserve to be treated like some saloon girl. She's YOUR wife. The woman you LOVE and she is having a baby! YOUR baby! The voice of reason scolded him, over and over again, until finally the realization of what he'd done hit him like a bullet to the heart.

"A baby! Abby is having *my* baby!" Gabe did a gig then hooted as loud as he could, so anyone within hearing distance could hear him. "I'm going to be a papa!"

Pouring more water into his hand, he stroked Spade's long sleek neck. "I've done something wrong, boy, horribly wrong. Taken the coward's way out."

Gabe shoved the canteen back into a saddlebag then mounted his horse and turned him south on the trail. Tapping his heels into the horse's side, Gabe urged him into a jog. He needed to get home before the love of his life grew frantic.

Love? Yes, I do love her and will till the day I die and beyond. And I'll love any child that comes from it.

If there was anything he knew, it was that he had to either get back to Abby or find a place to bed down for the night. The latter wasn't an option in his mind. Gabe buried his heels into Spade, sending him off at a lope. The ground flew under him as the sun disappeared under the horizon.

The gray dusk gave way to the coming darkness of the night. Gabe slowed the black horse to a walk as the road in front of him blended into the ground. Even with the full moon and cloudless night, the promise of little light made him cautious. No sense ruining a fine horse due to carelessness.

The aroma of a campfire reached his senses before Gabe saw it burning. Approaching slow and easy, dried brush crunching under his boots, he recognized the snow-white gelding belonging to the man putting a coffee pot over the fire—Bass Reeves.

"Hawkins, what brings you out here?" Reeves asked without looking up. Instead he reached for another cup, filling it with the steaming brew.

"And here I thought I was being quiet." Gabe loosened the cinch of his saddle then tied Spade next to the white horse. A stunning contrast— the black and white standing next to each other in peace.

"Tried too hard." Reeves handed Gabe the warm cup, the rich aroma filling his senses.

"Thanks." Gabe sat, drinking the brew, thankful for the warming it provided flowing to his belly.

"What brings you out?" Reeves poked the fire, stirring the embers into the air a few inches like little fire bugs.

Gabe thought for a moment. How much should he tell the U.S. Marshal? Should he reveal he ran from his wife because he was afraid to be a papa?

"Speak plainly, Hawkins. There's no one out here but the two of us."

"Do you have any children, Reeves?"

Reeves looked up at him through the smoke. "Yes, sir. Mighty proud of my youngin's."

"How do you handle it? Your wife—"

"My Nellie loves our babies, and me when I can make it home. Being a family man is hard on a marshal. The rewards outweigh the danger. I keep my family and your family safe, as well as the people in this territory. Isn't that why you became a lawman, Hawkins? To keep others safe? To ensure your loved ones are safe?"

"Yes, sir, I reckon when it comes right down to it."

"Then I suggest you get yourself back to your lovely wife, as she must be concerned. Just head on down the trail five miles and you'll be there."

Gabe stood, tossing the rest of his coffee into a bush. "I think I'll do just that, Reeves."

Gabe walked over to Spade, tightening the cinch around his belly. When he looked up, he stared into a pair of dark eyes.

"I'll need you one day soon, Hawkins."

"I'm sure you will. Right now I need my wife." Gabe perched himself in the saddle and pointed his horse's head south. With a swift kick of his heels, the beast took off into a lope.

He'd get home tonight and into Abby's loving embrace or die trying.

The sun disappeared behind the dark line of the horizon. The cheerful colors of sunset did little to uplift the heaviness of Abby's heart.

Gabe hadn't come back since riding out shortly before supper. Abby had continued with preparing the meal, confident her shocked husband would return within the hour once he'd cleared his mind.

But he hadn't.

It appeared he wouldn't be anytime soon either. The man her heart told her was true and strong rode away as soon as a child came into their lives. Abby clutched her stomach. How could she have misjudged him so? Yet her heart, through the betrayal of his abandonment, remained true to their love. While common sense told her he was never coming back, her heart believed he loved her too much not to come home. That deep down he would love their child.

When dusk finally gave way to the night, all hope Abby had clung to began to fade. She must accept she was left behind, expecting a child to raise on her own. Gabe, the man she trusted and loved, for reasons she may never know, had deserted her and their unborn babe.

The cloudless night and bright full moon did little to shed light on the trail leading from Fred. The only sounds were those of the creatures of the night. An owl hooted to a mate. A lonely coyote yipped a mournful tune.

No hoofbeats.

No Gabe riding back home.

"May you find your happiness, Gabriel Hawkins. God willing, I have found mine in the months since we wed. Our child is a gift of that love." Abby pushed out from the rocking chair she'd dragged out of the house and onto the porch hours earlier.

She returned to the darkness of the cabin and lit a small fire in the hearth. The supper of biscuits, beans and ham, now as cold as a Wisconsin winter day, sat on the stove top. She covered and stowed the food into the pantry, having no appetite. In the morning, she knew she'd need to eat and make a trip to the trading post.

Retrieving a piece of precious stationary from her lap desk, she sat fireside and began penning a letter to her friend, Rose.

My dear Rose,

We arrived safely in Fred, which has a trading post and a few homes. Ours is a three-room cabin vacated by another family long before we settled in. Up the road from us is the Cook family. Mr. Cook and his brother own the trading post in Fred. Mr. Cook's wife, Millie, paid me a visit with a warm pot of beans and ham. I am grateful to have a generous woman nearby. The Cooks are from Kentucky and have made their home here in this unsettled territory—and so shall I.

Deputy U.S. Marshal Bass Reeves paid Gabe a visit the day after we'd arrived. He is a fine man, and I believe has a good heart and soul. After several minutes, Gabe and Marshal Reeves were talking as if they'd known each other for a long time. The war that took so many souls must truly be over when a Confederate soldier and a former slave can take coffee together.

Our journey through Indian Territory was long and hot. We saw one cattle drive and it was magnificent. The beasts blew up such a spread of dust I thought there was a cyclone on the horizon. Mr. Cyrus Kennedy was out chasing down a few strays when he approached us. Mr. Kennedy was on his way to Dodge City to meet with Logan. He seems a kindly man and I believe Logan will find him agreeable.

Many nights we slept in the wagon with the canvas drawn back in hopes of a cool night breeze. The days were hot and exhausting. Bathing was done in a stream or pond we happened upon. The heat was unbearable at times. Except for the one time I took ill and we stopped for a few hours, we survived without any mishaps along the way.

I don't know how to say this except to just say it outright. I am with child! I am sure that the babe was conceived along our journey. There is an extra room that will serve as the baby's room and is large enough for the child to grow up in. I am thankful that I have this child, as it is the only one I'll likely ever be blessed with.

It is with heavy heart that I must tell you Gabe has left me now that I am with child. Don't think unkindly of him, Rose. He had only wanted a wife and thought he'd married one that would remain childless. He is a man with much on his mind and soul, so much sadness from the war. I believe he is an honorable man, even though my current situation shows otherwise. Like Robert, Gabe will always hold a place in my heart for I have loved no man more than he. Our babe is proof of that love.

Have no pity for me as this is the path laid out before me. I will send you word in the spring and introduce you to my daughter or son. The woman I spoke of, Millie Cook, is nearby and I am sure will be of great comfort to me.

There is a peacefulness in this untamed land that is hard to describe.

Give my love to Logan and Lilly.
You devoted friend,
Abby Hawkins

Abby placed her pen and paper into her desk, making a mental note to go to Cook's and drop off the letter in the morning. Dousing the fire, she checked to make sure the door was closed tightly, and then retired to the loneliness of her bed. Slipping into her nightdress, she curled up in the blankets, missing the warmth of Gabe's body next to her. Draping an arm across the spot where he would have laid, Abby cried herself to sleep.

Gabe hastily put Spade in the lean-to, tossing the saddle over the side of the wagon. After seeing to the mules and his tired horse, Gabe closed the door, protecting the livestock from coyotes.

The cabin was dark and unwelcoming, and no smoke came from the chimney as he rode up. What did he expect? That Abby would leave a lantern burning as she waited on the porch for him to return?

He stood at the bottom of the porch weighing his options. He could sleep in the chair on the porch or by the fireplace in the cabin until morning and hope with all his might Abby would not banish him. Or he could go to Abby as she lay in their bed, hold her close, and beg for her forgiveness.

Gabe wasn't afraid of much. He'd faced many an outlaw, the Union army, the rejection of his own flesh and blood; when it came to Abby he couldn't face the rest of his life without her. Without their child.

He stepped upon the porch and silently opened the door, peering into the darkness. A few small embers still burned in the hearth. Striking a match, Gabe lit a lantern, illuminating the room in a soft golden glow.

Abby's writing desk sat upon a chair near the hearth. His heart pounded in hopes it hadn't been long ago Abby had been sitting there. A piece of her plain writing paper and a lead pencil lay on top of the lap desk. Gabe picked up the letter and began reading about their journey, their nights spent in the wagon, and the cattle drive they came across. He smiled at Abby's words, remembering the day she'd fallen ill and how scared he'd been that he was going to lose her.

But it was the words she wrote of the baby where his heart soared only to crash when he read, "Gabe has left me." He'd failed her, plain and simple. Had he lost her this time around because of his fear?

The door to their bedroom wasn't latched shut, but he couldn't bring himself to venture in. The silence in the cabin was like a dark cave—cold. Nothing moved inside or outside the walls. It was as if no beings existed, save for himself.

Turning down the lantern, Gabe prepared to sleep in the lean-to. As he passed their bedroom, he heard soft whimpering and his heart shattered completely. Tentatively, he held his breath and pushed the door open. In not much more than a whisper he called her name. "Abby?"

She didn't stir, just continued to softly cry, curled up in the dark. He'd caused this. His loving wife whimpering in the night, his pillow grasped in her arms. Her back to him, she looked like a child.

Gabe sat next to her and gathered her in his arms. Her tears stained the sleeve of his shirt. Her swollen eyes blinked several times and then a tentative smile curled at the corners of her mouth.

"Gabe," she whispered before pushing out of his arms and swiping at her tear stained face. "You've come home."

"Yes. Will you ever forgive me? I've been such a fool. I was willing to lose everything that was good in my life. Willing to throw our love away because I was afraid."

"Afraid of what? Being a father?"

"Afraid of losing a child and becoming my parents. Afraid of not being the father our child deserves. Afraid of loving completely without regard to myself."

"Gabe—"

"Shh, let me finish. I love you beyond this place and time. I couldn't go on to be half the man I'd be without you in my life, Abby."

"But the baby—"

"Will be loved by both his mother and father. He'll grow to know right from wrong. He'll not be afraid to give his love freely as I have been until you became my wife—my life. He'll one day marry and give us grandchildren to dote on in our graying years."

"A son?" Abby laughed, the pillow still a barrier separating them.

"Yes, a son." Gabe pushed a stray strand of hair from Abby's face. The moonlight illuminating her soft features. *How did I get so lucky as to have married such an incredible woman?*

"What if it is a girl?"

"Then she'll be just as her mother is. Strong. Determined. And loved beyond life itself."

"Then come, lay next to me and show our baby how much you love her."

Gabe pulled off his boots and jeans. As he slid in next to Abby and held her tight in his arms, he knew the world was right again. This is where he was meant to be, holding Abby. Loving Abby. Forever and always with Abby.

"I love you, Abigail Hawkins," he whispered, kissing her neck and then that sweet spot behind her ear. "Will you find it in your heart to forgive me?"

"Oh, quick, give me your hand." Abby placed his hand over her belly, pressing it gently over the center of the small rounded swell of her belly. After a few moments he felt it, a flutter like the wings of a young bird.

"Can you feel that?"

"Is that…?"

"I think so."

Gabe let the tears seep from his eyes as he smothered his face into Abby's hair. His hand never left his wife's stomach as they fell into a peaceful sleep.

CHAPTER EIGHT

Three Months Later

Abby rinsed then scrubbed a muslin chemise from her tub of laundry. The darkening water splashed onto her apron with each dunk, swish, and wringing out of the item. Satisfied with its cleanliness, she placed it over the rope Gabe had strung across the end of the porch for her to hang the wet laundry on. In the warm southern breeze, it wouldn't take long for the garment to dry.

Sliding the undergarment across the rope, she smiled. Their baby reacted to the pair of arms gently coming around her swollen belly.

"How's our boy doing this morning?" Gabe whispered in her ear, his voice soft and loving. In a matter of months Gabe had become a doting husband. He'd taken extreme interest in making furniture to turn their cabin into a home for the baby. A small cradle made of pine now sat next to their bed in wait. He'd even fashioned a pie safe from broken crates he'd retrieved from the trading post. As much as she enjoyed his attention to her needs, she longed for some time to herself. She had many things to do with the babe due in a few short months.

"Our little one is active this morning. I think she wants to come out and play." Abby turned, gazing into her husband's eyes. "Like her papa, she's impatient."

"Or he's still hungry." Gabe knelt, pressing his lips to the spot where the baby just rolled. Abby loved this time of morning when he said hello to their baby, whispering words only the babe heard. Words meant for their child; a private conversation between a papa and his unborn child.

"Well, then, now that that is settled." Gabe stood, capturing Abby in his arms. "Have you completed the wash? I want to go see Walter Cook, but not until I know you are finished for the day. The last thing I want is you trying to empty the washtub on your own. I'll not have my wife doing man's work when you're this far along with child."

"Yes, I'm done—for today." Abby kissed Gabe fully. Desire welled inside her, reminding her of how powerful their love had been in the early morning hours before dawn.

"You keep doin' that and I'll never get to the post," Gabe teased, releasing her.

It was always the same; the emptiness she felt when he let go of her. She'd never tire of feeling the hollowness when not in his arms; to her it meant their love was deep and strong.

Abby stood at the doorway watching Gabe lug the half-full washtub to the end of the cabin to empty the dirty water into her flowerbed. Carrying the tub in his arms, his muscles rippled under the rolled-up sleeves of the cotton shirt. He'd become strong as an ox since leaving Dodge City. There was more labor involved here in the wilderness then walking down the street to the

Dodge House or over to the train station to welcome the passengers into town.

Over the past several months Gabe had cleared and tilled a small space of dirt for a garden where she grew onions, potatoes, and various herbs that took to the red dirt. One day he even surprised her by clearing a path around the cabin and planting some flowers for her.

As there wasn't much in the way of crime or outlaws riding into Fred, he'd set about repairing the cabin and lean-to for the winter months with wood from the trees he and Walter Cook chopped down. Her city husband had become a strong and dedicated homesteader—Abby couldn't be any happier.

Abby strolled back into the cabin, leaving the inside door open now that there was a screen door. Gabe had fashioned one and put it up after her complaining she needed fresh air through the house and not wanting to leave the door opened wide enough for unwanted creatures to venture inside.

The fixings Gabe had retrieved from the pantry for a cake sat on the table. The flour bag didn't weigh more than three pounds, but Gabe wouldn't allow her to lift anything now that the baby grew and her belly swelled under her clothing. She wouldn't dream of asking him to lift or do for her as long as she was still capable of doing for herself. But since that night three months ago he'd been protective—overly protective. Abby never mentioned anything about his actions, but figured what he didn't know wouldn't hurt him.

Sieving the flour, sugar, and baking soda into the bowl, Abby worked a pound of butter into the dry mixture. Pouring a pint of water into the bowl, she hummed *Camptown Races* as she melded the ingredients into a cake batter for tonight's dessert.

A horse's neigh drew her attention. She looked up,

expecting to see Spade tied to the porch rail. Instead she watched Marshal Reeves step upon their porch, black hat in hand, then knock upon the screen door.

"Sorry to bother you so early in the morning, Mrs. Hawkins. Is your husband about?" The lawman waited, his eyes dark and serious, brows furrowed in thought. This was not the happy-go-lucky man she'd grown accustomed to and welcomed at their dinner table more than once over the past few months.

"Yes, Bass, he's probably down by the stream fetchin' some water or in the barn tending to the animals." Abby dusted off her hands and walked to the door, pushing it open. "There's hot coffee and leftover biscuits and gravy, if you'd like come sit and have some until Gabe comes in."

"No, thank you, ma'am. I'm here on official business this time." Reeves declined, staying outside the door for the first time in his many unexpected visits.

"What kind of business, Reeves?" Gabe stood at the bottom of the porch, unrolling his shirt sleeves.

The U.S. marshal glanced at Abby through the screen then turned to Gabe. "Official. I'll wait for you by the water trough while my horse takes his fill, if that is right by you."

Gabe nodded, then smiled at Abby before joining the marshal. She pushed open the door, her heart pounding like native drums in the night. Pretending to check the laundry on the line, she watched Gabe and Bass huddled in a private conversation.

Gabe nodded, said something she couldn't hear, then looked over at her. Every fear she never knew she had stumbled through her.

Gabe was being called to duty.

"Do you know where the Evans gang is, Bass?" Gabe handed the deputy U.S. marshal a bucket of oats for his horse, his hand trembling but from what he wasn't sure. Fear? Or the possibility of actually doing what he was trained to do—bring down the outlaws in this lawless haven criminals took refuge in.

"Lost them between here and the mountains to the southwest. I've been on their trail for months. Word is they heard of a stagecoach coming through with a strongbox containing bank notes. I've got a Creek scout looking for their trail, but..." Bass stroked the neck of the gelding, letting the horse get his fill of the sweet oat mix.

"You figure they're headed here? There's not a stage due for a good month or more that I know of," Gabe stated, unsure if Bass's information was correct or not. It could be a setup by Jesse Evans, knowing the U.S. marshal was on his trail. And the information could be months old, if it was good. Anything could happen to change the plans of a traveler from the East.

"I had a telegram sent to the Pinkerton detective, Logan Granger. A hired stage left three days ago out of Dodge City. A rich businessman and his family from out East going to Texas. Heard there's quite the bank roll in the strongbox, as well as silver." Bass loosened the cinch of the saddle, then pulled some jerky from a saddlebag.

Gabe thought for a moment, trying to remember if he'd heard rumor of anyone heading to Dodge City before they'd left but couldn't. Six months was a long while to remember what happened in a world now foreign to him.

"How do I get word to you if they ride into these parts?" Gabe offered a ladle of water to Bass, watching his expression. But as usual, the marshal gave nothing away.

Bass peered over the top of the ladle, looking Gabe square in the eye. Right then and there, in the brief moment, Gabe knew he wasn't going to like the answer.

"I'll require you to ride with me. I already spoke to Walter Cook. He'll be nearby and send word should you need to return." Bass re-tightened the cinch then handed the empty feed bucket and ladle over to Gabe. "Gabe, we could be on their trail for several weeks. I want to get them before that stage gets too far into Indian Territory."

Gabe swallowed the lump in his throat, one of his greatest fears coming to fruition. His mind raced to find a reason, any reason, for him to stay. A reason to decline a request from his fellow lawman and found none that would make him out to be anything less cowardly.

If he used Abby and the baby as a reason to stay behind he'd be seen as that coward and it would pose more danger than not. The way Gabe saw it, he had no choice but to go with Reeves.

"How long do I have before we leave?" Gabe glanced toward the house, feeling Abby's gaze upon him.

"Out of respect for Mrs. Hawkins, whom I've grown fond of, the morning will be soon enough." Bass remounted the gray, adjusting himself in the saddle. "Say your goodbyes, I'll be back at sunrise."

Gabe nodded, "Fair enough."

"Well then, until the sun rises." Bass rode off, leaving Gabe with a hole in his gut.

The time he thought he'd have with Abby until their son was born now gone, Gabe turned toward the cabin to find her waiting for him on the porch.

"Lord, give me the strength to leave my love in her time of need," he muttered, then strolled across the yard.

"You're leaving," Abby stated, folding the clothes as she pulled them from the rope one by one.

"Yes." Gabe looked away from the fear in her eyes, his steadfastness waning.

"How soon?" Abby dropped the last of the day's wash into the basket.

"Sunrise," Gabe stated, watching her shoulders draw back.

Abby smiled despite the tears he saw welling in her brown eyes. "Then come inside. We have much to do before we say a proper farewell," she said, extending her hand to him.

Gabe leapt upon the porch, pulling her into his arms. The scent of lavender lingering in Abby's hair filled his mind until it was stamped firmly into his memory. The swell of her belly where their child lay in wait against him was a stealth reminder of his reasons for whom he'd become to Abby. To himself.

The woman made him a better man. The love of his life made him face his fears with love, understanding, and courage. Abby, his wife, his everything.

And now he silently called upon her to show him the courage within to leave her and their unborn baby. To ride off in the morning. To answer the call of duty to protect those unable to protect themselves.

"Abby," he whispered into long brown strands of hair cascading over her shoulders. He found her mouth with his, kissing her with passion he didn't know lived within him.

With a hand in hers, Gabe allowed her to take him through the cabin door and across the floor to their bedroom. Slowly he undressed her, his hands skimming lightly over her heated skin. Their child moved beneath his hand as it danced inside her belly.

Abby worked the buttons on his jeans, then slid them just past his hips. Gabe kicked off his boots, then yanked his jeans completely off, leaving them in a clump on the floor before lying next to Abby.

Gathering her into his arms, Gabe held her close, her softness kissing his work-worn skin, igniting his senses.

Gooseflesh prickled her body as his lips traveled a path over her face, down her long, silky neck, and over breasts swelling with nourishment for the baby. Her fingertips tracked lines over his back, sending jagged edges of desire through him.

No words of love were needed.

No false promises spoken aloud.

Only the promise of love, need, want, and desire between a man and his wife.

In the early morning hours before the sun rose in the east, Abby rocked slowly back and forth in the porch chair, reflecting on the past several hours. Their lovemaking during the night had been sweet, even lustful at times, but it might be the last time she would feel Gabe next to her. Somehow, she'd have to come to terms with it. She'd have to be strong, not let him see her worries.

When he rode out in a few hours, she needed him to see that she loved him and would wait no matter how long.

The hours before dawn were cool and Abby pulled the knitted shawl tighter around her shoulders. A courting song of a robin sent chills down her spine. Much like Gabe in the moonlit night, the songbird sought out its mate with music—sweet and full of promise.

She shut her eyes recording to memory Gabe's touch. How the roughness of his hands felt like silk upon her skin. The gooseflesh sprinkled across her body when he'd slipped her dress from her followed by the chemise.

The heat from his lips set her on fire with each touch. His whispered words of love upon her ear made her blood race with desire. Her fingers fumbling with the buttons of his blue denim pants in her haste to bed her husband before the morning came to take him from her.

His words soft as he spoke to their unborn child. Telling tales to the babe of his life before the War Between the States and life on a southern plantation. He told their child of how he'd been swept away the first time he'd seen her. How much he loved both Abby and the baby. That he wished the baby, if a boy, to be named James Gabriel Stewart Hawkins, after his father. He told the restless baby the importance of family, of standing up for what was right in the world, that above all else to be lawful and true to those around him. Of not being afraid to give his heart to the right woman when the time was right.

"One day our child must learn to read and write, and go to a university, Abby. He'll travel to faraway places and experience life as we've never been able," he told her, gazing onto her face with need for her to make his wishes come true. Abby had nodded her promise, tears sliding down her cheeks.

"I'll be right here waiting for you no matter how long it takes." She made the promise with more tears on the edge of her lashes and a small weak smile on her lips.

"The boy will need a father, Abby. Promise me you'll find a good man with a loving hand to care for you and the child should I not return."

"There'll be no need as he'll have no father other than you. There'll be no other. I'll not expect nothing less of you, my husband—my love and my life." Abby kissed him with renewed passion in her body and fear of never seeing him again clutching her heart. "That I can be sure of, and I'll not promise otherwise Gabe."

He'd returned her kiss then and they'd made love by the moonlight streaming through the bedroom window until they both were spent and fell asleep wrapped around each other.

She brought to mind the song of his snoring as she lay awake, wrapped in his arms, tears staining her pillow. His fingers flexing around her arm as he slept, making sure she was still there. The murmurs from a dream he wouldn't remember having come morning.

Abby planned on growing old with Gabe at her side. She'd dreamed of him playing with their child and grandchildren. Of Gabe teaching them how to ride bareback across the plains. Her child, their baby, might never be held by or know its father. How much he loved it. But she'd make darn sure their child grew to know him.

The baby stirred, drawing Abby from of her musings, reminding her there was much to be done before Bass Reeves returned at sunrise. Tears trickled down her cheeks as she stored her memories safely away.

Swiping back the tears of self-pity, she returned to the cabin and packed baked goods into a sack. She'd risen long before her husband to prepare the biscuits and small cakes for his journey. She wanted him to take a little piece of home with him.

CHAPTER NINE

"Abby," he said in a sleepy tone, rolling over, wanting his wife when all he found was a cold empty space. Springing to his feet, he snatched his pants off the floor and up over his legs and hips, then ventured out into the front room buttoning his fly. Pausing for a moment he took in the sweet vision before him.

The white cotton gown left little to douse his growing desire. If it were at all possible, Abby was more beautiful at the simplest of times.

What was it about a woman first thing in the morning before the household moved about? Abby stirred a deep need in him. He yearned to take her in his arms and make love to her until Reeves came banging on the door. Until he had to leave her in her hours of need to hunt down a gang of outlaws. For the first time since arriving in Fred and Indian Territory, Gabe wished they were still in Dodge City where his jurisdiction didn't include the entire territory of Kansas.

"Are you going to stand there all day gawking like a silly schoolboy?" Abby turned, a smile on her face. In the moments it took him to cross the few feet to her, the gown lay in a pool at her feet. "Stop right there," she commanded, a hand upon the swell where his son grew strong each day.

"Gawd, woman," Gabe hissed, the temperature in his body rising like the heat of a summer day in July. "Do you have any idea what you are doing?"

"Take a long look my love. Draw my image to mind when you need to remember what waits for you at home." Arms open wide, Abby pivoted on one foot then bent down, slowly drawing her gown over her nakedness. Walking back to the bedroom, she lingered long enough to place a hand where his heart thundered like a herd of mustangs. Smiling, she continued back to the bedroom closing the door behind her.

Gabe fought the urge to follow her. To make love to Abby as if it were for the last time. However, if he did he knew in his heart that she'd look in his eyes and know he didn't expect to make it back home in one piece, if at all. Staring at the closed door he debated throwing caution to the wind.

"Hell with it," he muttered, mind made up. Stepping to the door, his hand raised to knock, asking for entry.

As his knuckles were about to rap on the barrier, the door opened. Abby stood in the gray light of day snaking through the window. She wore her best dress and her brown hair was piled upon her head. She looked as she had the day he'd fallen for her. The day she'd stood on the train platform in Dodge City.

"Are you going somewhere?" Gabe's admiration quickly turned to suspicion. She'd not worn that dress since the day they were married, and she had her receptacle in one hand and the matching bonnet in the other. All that was missing was her travel jacket.

"Yes, I'll need to go and get supplies at the trading

post once you've left. You'll be riding out soon and there is no way I'm going to wait for someone to bring what is needed." Abby smiled, then walked past him to the table. "I've got some things—"

"You aren't going anywhere! I'll not have my wife walk a mile to the post and back with an arm full of provisions," Gabe's nostrils flared and he bared his teeth. Gabe was furious with her. What possessed her to even consider wandering about unattended? Was she daft? Where has his levelheaded wife gone? She certainly was not standing before him.

"Be that as it may, I am not a helpless woman." Abby smiled slightly, but he saw the fire in her eyes. "Walking is good for the baby and will make childbirth easier on both of us."

"That's a bunch of hogwash and you know it." Gabe crossed the floor planks to her then stood over the table, hands spread out in front of him. If he kept them there he might not grab and shake some sense into her. "There is a gang of ruthless outlaws heading this way. It's far too dangerous for you, or Millie, to be prancing between here and the trading post."

"And what do you think Millie did before the great lawman Gabe Hawkins came to town? Do you think for one minute she sat on the porch waiting for Walter to bring supper home?" Abby stood hands on hips, her head high in defiance.

Gabe knew that look on her face. She wouldn't easily back down, even so he had to try and make her understand the element of danger that gang posed. She had to see going to the trading post could put her life in danger as well as his son's chance to come into this world.

"If the Evans gang does come this way with no law around to fight them— well, it won't be pretty. They'll most likely loot everything at Cook's," Gabe stated coming around behind her. "Lord knows what they'd do to two helpless women and a young boy with only Walter here to defend you."

"I'm not about to stay holed up in the cabin for Lord knows how long while you are out there doing your job. Do you really think by doing so it's going to stop them from barging in our home if they want to? Or stop them from taking the mules? No, Gabe, it's not!" Abby turned facing him, her gaze boring a hole into his soul.

"Mr. Hawkins, I'll have you remember you were a lawman long before you were my husband. I'll not have you forget that ever." Abby fell into Gabe's arms her tears on the edge of her lashes. "Don't you dare treat me like a child with no sense of my own."

"Mrs. Hawkins, I am now and always will be your husband and protector above all else. I'll not have you forget *that*," he said pressing her against him. His lips sought hers, kissing her hard with an urgency of a man fearful of never seeing his love again. "I'll not have you forget how much I love you."

Gabe held on a moment longer then willed himself to let Abby go. A tear slipped down her face. He brushed it away with the pad of a thumb.

"Come now, I need to go to the lean-to. Spade needs his oats before I leave or he'll be trying to eat every bush along the way." Gabe smiled then turned to the door. Before he got half the distance, he was hit from behind by a shirt in the head. "I stand firm Abby, you'll not leave this cabin for anything!"

"You may want to finish dressing first," Abby hissed, slamming the bedroom door.

Gabe shook his head, pulling the garment down over his shoulders and walked out the door. The sun was beginning its rise above the eastern horizon. Reeves would be there soon and he had things to do.

Spade ate from the bucket of oats as Gabe ran a brush over his back. "Damn woman! Does she think there's a peace officer around every corner? This is not Dodge City, it's Indian Territory. Unsettled and untamed. She'd can't go strolling down the road as if it were a summer Sunday morning."

Gabe tossed the horse blanket followed by the saddle over his horse's back and withers. Spade tossed his head and stomped a foot. The black was ready to move on; he'd been confined to the two miles it took to get to the trading post and back. Gabe hadn't gone far from the cabin or his family himself for the past three months. He wouldn't be doing it now except...

Now he had an obligation to not only protect his wife, but to chase after outlaws hell bent on robbing a stagecoach. He doubted the outcome would be a good one.

Abby paced the floor of the bedroom, wearing a path on the planks leading to nowhere except from words raised in frustration. She shouldn't have provoked Gabe, but she wasn't going to let him ride away worrying about her. At least not any more than he already did.

A red ring was beginning to form around her wrists the more she rubbed them. Her body trembled as she tried to keep from bursting into tears.

"Lord, have I done the right thing?" she muttered, clenching her hands into fists then relaxing them. "What if he doesn't come back and we've parted ways in anger? It'll be all my fault if he dies thinking—"

Unable to hold back the tears any longer, Abby fell upon the bed where they'd made love through the night.

The sweetness of that farewell now tainted by her trickery to make him believe she would be strong without him there.

In truth, she was scared. Scared of losing the man she cherished above all others. Gabe was the love of her life, she knew that now. She'd probably known it in her heart from the day she laid eyes on his face.

At one time she may have been a strong woman long before she ever came to know him. Since falling under Gabe's protection and love, Abby had let all that false strength slip away. There had been no need to pretend any more.

Until yesterday when she called upon the false strength once more for the sake of their child. To convince Gabe she'd be safe while he performed his duty as a lawman.

"Now what do I do?" Her gaze bounced across the room as if the answer were there hiding in wait for her to find it.

Abby stood, smoothing back a few loose strands of hair. "If I tell him of my false proclamation he'll ride away worrying. That worry could cause his judgment to waiver. On the other hand, if I keep my secret he rides out angry with me, but hopeful I will be able to withstand his absence."

Opening the bedroom door, she got her writing desk from near the fireplace and sat at the table. Lifting the lid, she removed a piece of stationary.

My Dearest Husband,

When I arrived in Dodge City to meet a man I'd been exchanging letters with, I did not expect to love you. Against the dark emptiness I thought was in my heart, I do love you more than I thought I would.

From the moment you stepped upon the platform I

knew in my heart I was meant to be your wife. And though our wedding was in haste and under my silent protest, I have never been happier than to be at your side.

You have given me more in life than I could have hoped for, as I thought I'd never find someone to love again. You are a man who made me love you. You have given me a child I never thought I'd have. A family I've missed for far too many years.

I answered your advertisement to escape the daily reminder of my sorrow. I'd hoped, no prayed, that you'd truly have a kind heart. In these months I've learned that you have so much more.

You, my dear Gabe, are a man who loves deeply and completely. A man who faces his fears and resolves to not let them take you over. Do not let the fear of my welfare while you chase outlaws control you. You will control it. I have faith in you.

I played a dirty trick on you for sure. I let you ride away believing I am strong and can take care of whatever comes. In truth, I am scared you won't return to me. That our child will never know his father. Yes, my love, I said his father.

Know that I will not let that fear control me either. I believe deep in my heart that you will return. I believe our love is stronger than the fear inside us, that is where I'll draw my strength and courage from.

Never let my image out of your heart, as I will never let our last night together out of mine.

Return to me as I will be here waiting for you until my dying day. James and I wait for the sound of Spade carrying you home to us.

Your loving wife,
Abby

Swiping the tears from her eyes, Abby folded the paper in half then slipped it into an envelope to protect it. She closed her writing desk at the sound of a horse and rider approaching their porch.

Bass Reeves had come to take her husband away with him.

"Morning."

Gabe looked up from putting the last bit of hay up for Abby. Bass stood in the lean-to door, reins in his hand, hat pulled down over his eyes. The morning sun was already making its heated rise into the eastern sky.

"Have you had breakfast yet?" Gabe asked ambling over to the marshal, Spade's headstall in his hand.

"Coffee and a hard biscuit a few hours back," Bass answered, dusting red dirt from his black hat.

"Where'd you spend the night? From the looks of it you didn't get much sleep." Gabe took note of the lines edging the marshal's bloodshot dark eyes.

"A Creek camp for a bit, then moved out before day broke through the darkness," Bass settled his big black hat over the saddle horn.

Gabe nodded then strolled back to his horse, slipping the bit into its mouth and the headstall over its ears. "You got a plan yet?"

"Thought maybe we could go over it while eatin' your wife's fine fried eggs and biscuits and gravy. I sure could use a damn good cup of coffee instead of the sludge I put in my gut." Bass grinned, his eyes full of hope for some of Abby's home cooking.

"It's been a rough morning, not sure what kind of company my wife will be in." Gabe lead his horse out the barn, tying it to the porch rail. As much as he trusted and liked Bass, family disputes between a man and his wife was nobody's business but the husband's. "Not even sure if she's begun to think about putting food on the table, let alone set coffee to brewing."

Bass smiled, slapping Gabe on the back. "Nothin' a bit of sugar won't fix. The nicer the bee, the sweeter the honey I always say."

"I wouldn't be too sure of that," Gabe said glancing toward the door, seeing the look on Abby's face when she'd stormed away from him angry as a hornet's nest. The darn woman, God love her, was going to defy him as sure as the sun rises in the morning and sets at night. He prayed she'd hold her tongue in front of the marshal.

Gabe proceeded with caution across the porch, pausing at the screen door and peered inside. Abby had changed into a day dress and stood over the stove with her apron tied around her waist. Cracking followed by the savory scent of bacon from the fry pan she stood over wafted in the air. Damn she was a beautiful sight angry or not.

"If you're wanting to eat before y'all leave then you might wanna get yourself at the table before these bacon and eggs are cold," she called out, not once turning to look at him.

He glanced over his shoulder in time to see the snicker leave Bass's face. Pushing open the door, Gabe noticed the bulging flour sack slumped against the wall. *Were his clothes or provisions in that bag?* he wondered, picking up the sack and feeling the contents.

At least she's not going to let me starve, he thought as a bit of relief seeped into his veins. It appeared there was a cease-fire administered for this battle, but what about the war he was sure would come eventually? Would it be worth the words said in anger they'd never be able to take back? Gabe thought not. In his mind, his wife had won this time—he just wasn't going to let her know it.

"Mornin', ma'am." Bass nodded taking a seat at the table. "Mighty fine of you offerin' up breakfast."

"Morning, Bass, nice to see you again considering the circumstance." Fry pan in hand, Abby smiled crossing over to the table then slid a fair share of bacon and eggs onto each plate. "I'll not have you both ride out of here on empty stomachs. Coffee will be ready in a minute."

Gabe looked up at his wife, noticing the red rims around her eyes and her pink nose. She'd been crying and it was because of him. Because of his bullheaded idea that she wasn't capable of taking care of herself. When will he ever learn to keep his mouth shut? When it came to protecting his family, probably never.

"My Nellie is of the same mind, Abby." Bass dug his fork into the eggs slurping a slice of bacon into the bright yellow yolks, then popped the gooey mess into his mouth. "Damn good food, pardon the cussin'."

"I've heard worse in my day, Bass, no need to apologize." Abby chuckled pouring more coffee into the half-full cups. "I suspect I'll hear darn near every cuss word there is before I'm laid in the ground. Might even say one or two myself when the baby decides to come out into the world."

"You said you had a plan?" Gabe hated not knowing what he was riding into. No lawman should go chasing outlaws without an idea of what he'd planned to do. He'd always had a well thought out plan of attack even for the gunslingers that came through Dodge City. Granted, they were in uncivilized territory, but Gabe believed a plan of action had to be well thought out even if it changed mid-stream.

"Yes, sir. I reckon to catch up with that private stage afore it gets too far into Indian Territory." Bass took a swig of the fresh coffee, a smile spreading across his face. "There'll be two more passengers that Jesse Evans hadn't counted on. Armed passengers."

Gabe pushed back his empty plate and stared across the table. "And just how do you propose that?"

"Well, sir, with the grace of God and our wits."

Gabe's gaze sprung over to Abby's face, registering the fear in her eyes. This was not going to have a good outcome. He could feel it in his bones.

CHAPTER TEN

Abby refused to allow the tears burning her eyes to fall. She stood planted on the porch as Gabe tied the flour sack full of provisions onto a saddlebag. Her heart and mind cried out to run to him and hold on for dear life, while her body refused to move an inch.

Gabe hopped onto the porch and pulled her into his arms. Tears burst over the dam and flowed down her cheeks unabated. She buried her face into his chest afraid if she embraced him she'd all but beg him not to leave.

"Abby, I mean it. Do not go to the trading post while I'm gone." He held her at arm's length his eyes begging her to do as he asked. "Please stay at the cabin. I can't be worrying about you while I'm out there any more than I'm gonna anyway."

How could she defy her husband in front of the deputy U.S. marshal? She couldn't. More to the point she wouldn't embarrass him. Instead she wiped her eyes and nodded. "You just make sure you come home."

Gabe crushed her against his chest, his mouth sought hers bruising her lips with a desperate kiss. "I promise," his whispered pledge warm against her mouth.

"Hate to break up this tender moment, but daylight's burnin'." Bass urged his horse into a walk and headed northeast along the road.

Abby stepped out of Gabe's arms, backing away from him a step at a time. "You go. I'll be here when you get back."

Gabe nodded then mounted his black. "There's hay put down for ya. Walter will be by on his way home each night to see what you need the next day. I love you, Abigail Hawkins."

"I love you too, Gabriel Hawkins." She smiled, nervously wiping her hands down over her apron. Gabe tipped his hat then spurred his horse into a trot and moved out after Bass.

Abby watched from the porch until Gabe disappeared from her sight. Taking a deep breath to calm her quivering nerves, she went into the house and began cleaning up the breakfast dishes. She had to do something to keep from breaking down into tears.

Over the next several hours she set about cleaning the cabin. Sweeping floors, making their bed, putting up the clean clothes from yesterday's wash, all temporary distractions from the sorrow of Gabe's leaving. The cabin seemed unusually quiet without Gabe coming in and out to check on her, or bringing in water or eggs from the few chickens they had. The milk cow hadn't arrived yet, or he'd have been toting in fresh milk as well. Abby had never noticed his absence before—even when he'd gone to the post for supplics it hadn't seemed this quiet. Now it was nearly unbearable in the few hours since he rode away to face heaven knew what.

"If this is what it would be like without him for the rest of my life, I'd go plum crazy," she remarked, sweeping the ever-present red dirt from the porch. The more she swept it away, the more the southern wind laid the red substance upon the planks.

"No sense wearing ourselves out for no reason at all," Abby exhaustedly resolved, gliding a hand over her swollen belly, giggling when the baby kicked in agreement. "Ha, well then, it's settled. A glass of sweet tea and the rocking chair for us, little one."

Abby set the hot water and tea to brewing then pulled down the sack of sugar from a pantry shelf when the sound of wagon wheels drew her attention. Walking over to the screen door, she smiled seeing Millie Cook in a small one-horse carriage with the reins in her hands.

"Millie! You're in time for some tea. I hope you stay for some." Abby pushed open the door, clasping her hands to her chest. "I'm so happy to see you. It's been several days since you last came by. Please do stay, Millie. I could use a friend right about now."

"Tea sounds absolutely delicious." Millie lighted from the carriage, tying off the horse to the porch rail. "I'd love to stay for a bit. I've missed having another woman to talk to as well."

Abby went back inside and prepared two servings of sweet tea. With a cup in each hand, she pushed the door open with her hip and joined Millie on the porch. Millie had settled nicely into one of the two rocking chairs, fanning herself with a handkerchief.

"How's that baby of yours?" Millie smiled, taking a cup from Abby.

"Moving around more and more. Sometimes I think it will kick its way out." Abby laughed sitting in the rocker next to Millie, sipping the cooling amber liquid, relishing its sweetness as it cooled her rising body temperature. "I think Gabe is right. I was hoping for a girl, but I think it is a boy after all."

"Only the baby and the good Lord know for sure,

Abby." Millie said, experience edging her words. "Did you decide on a name yet?"

"Ha, James Gabriel Stewart Hawkins, if Gabe has his way." Abby shook her head, clucking. "I'd prefer just plain ol' Jimmy Hawkins, myself."

"That is a truly a mouthful for any youngster. Jimmy seems much easier for a child to remember," Millie agreed, rocking in a matching rhythm with Abby.

"It is Gabe's idea to name our son after his father. Even after all his family has gone through, he wants to honor them this way." Abby recited a bit of the Hawkins family history, leaving out the private sequence of events that had Gabe estranged from his parents. "I haven't thought of a girl's name yet."

"You best try, in case little Jimmy is a Janey!" Millie laughed, fanning the summer heat from her face.

Abby smiled, looking over at her friend. "Where you off to anyway?"

"Walter told me Gabe was leaving this morning and would be gone for a piece." Millie smiled, holding her cup of tea in her lap. "I was on my way to pick up Charlie and thought you might want to ride along in case there's supplies you'll be needing. Walter said he'd be stopping by every night, but if for nothing else it'll get you away from the cabin for a spell."

"Gabe was pretty stern on me staying here at the cabin. He doesn't want me going into Fred while these outlaws are on the loose for anything." Abby pondered her promise to her husband. She knew if he was going to be gone for an extended period of time she'd go absolutely crazy not seeing anyone. Plus, if something did happen and Gabe didn't return home, she'd have to know how to take care of herself.

The decision made Abby jumped at the chance to leave the confines of the cabin. "It might take me a bit to take inventory of the pantry. Do you have time?" Anything was better than sitting around feeling sorry for herself and worried if Gabe was in danger or not.

"I even have time for lunch if you'd a mind to it." Millie suggested.

"Then lunch it is before we go to the post." Abby agreed grateful for the company.

The two friends sat on the porch sipping sweet tea as leisurely as a couple of southern plantation ladies on a hot summer day. Not a care in the world, and no place they immediately had to be.

***

The sun rose to its highest point in the clear blue sky. Gabe glanced over at Bass, amazed neither he nor his horse looked any worse for the wear. Gabe was cooking under the heat of the summer sun. They'd been riding steady for the past few hours at an easy pace since leaving Cook's on their way out of Fred. While Bass had gathered a few items, Gabe took the opportunity in requesting Walter to look in on Abby.

"Mr. Cook gonna look in on the missus?" Bass asked keeping his head on the pivot he'd been doing for the past several hours. Between the two of them, there wasn't much they could miss. Unless of course a rattlesnake slithered out from under a bush then they'd both be on the ground with no horse under either of them.

"Yes, but he seemed pretty sure Abby will make her way to the trading post. Walter told his wife about our mission and that Abby would be home alone. He felt the two of them would come around sooner or later." Gabe chuckled, shaking his head. "Regardless of my asking her to stay at the cabin while I'm gone, I know Abby will find a way to the post—even if she has to walk. Damn independent woman that she is."

"Would you have it any other way? You don't seem the type of man who'd want a submissive woman on your hands."

"Damn right about that! Abby does challenge me, I'll give you that." Gabe puffed out his chest despite himself. He was proud, scared, worried all rolled into one emotion. Top that off with outlaws in the area he couldn't see any reason for living if anything happened to her.

"We should reach Silver City before long," Bass remarked, urging the gray into a trot. "The town sheriff there will keep an eye on that stage until we arrive. Once on board we'll head back on the stage road. Hopefully draw out the Evans gang."

Gabe nodded, unsure if that plan would work or not. Ideally the gang wouldn't be expecting two extra passengers. He doubted them riding along could deter the gang from robbing the stage. He didn't question Reeves' authority even if it raised questions in his mind without a solution of his own.

As the hours slipped by and the sun began to shift to the west, they rode into Silver City. Gabe and Bass pulled up in front of the jail, greeted by a less than enthusiastic sheriff. It was all too clear he didn't appreciate their presence.

"Marshal." The sheriff tipped his hat, his face anything less than friendly. It was obvious he didn't want a federal lawman, let alone two federal lawmen, walking the streets of his town.

"Sheriff Brown, this is Marshal Hawkins. He's been reassigned from Dodge City to Fred by Judge Parker." Bass introduced them and the sheriff reluctantly acknowledged Gabe.

"Humph, come on inside then, no sense standing out here discussin' business." Sheriff Brown turned on his heel, making no effort to wait on the lawmen who'd just ridden uninvited into his town. The mention of Judge Parker may have made the sheriff compliant. It didn't make him any friendlier.

Gabe followed Bass into the small office that housed one empty cell, then kept watch on the street from the doorway.

"What's this all about, Reeves? That stage could have been on its way with a fresh team of horses, now it's held up at the blacksmith's," the sheriff spat with a total disregard to rank.

"The Jesse Evans Gang is believed to be in the area. We received a report that private stage is their target and I aim to bring the gang into Fort Smith." Bass, to his credit, ignored the disrespect given a black man with a federal badge.

"I ain't seen no trace of those boys." Sheriff Brown sat down, swinging his feet on the desk. "They ain't got no call to come here."

"Listen sheriff, I understand how you feel," Gabe interjected from his post, the nonchalance of the sheriff grated on his sense of duty. "I felt that same way every time a federal marshal rode into Dodge. I had to remind myself why I put this badge on. Why that federal marshal pinned one on. To serve and protect the citizens of my district. That's the bottom line in my book."

The sheriff nodded then turned to Bass. "The man on that stage goes by the name of Douglas Manchester. He's got his wife and two youngin's with him. They're all dressed like dandies from the east. Have no business out here in my book."

Bass glanced at Gabe. Neither of them had expected an entire family. This wasn't what they'd planned for. It was enough to protect a wealthy East coast businessman, but his entire family?

"Who's drivin' the stage?" Gabe asked, hoping it was someone he knew from Dodge.

"A fellow by the name of Granger is riding shotgun, but he doesn't look the part." Sheriff Brown smirked, sliding his feet off the desk. "You'll find the lot of them over at the hotel."

"Thank you, sheriff. I'll be sure to let the judge know how you cooperated." Bass said, shaking the man's hand. "Let's go, Hawkins."

"Granger? Isn't that the Pinkerton from Dodge?" Bass asked as they untied their horses and walked across the street to the hotel.

"Yes, sir. I can't imagine what the hell Logan is doing here, but I aim to find out." Gabe handed off his reins to Bass, then stomped into the hotel lobby. Slapping the trail dust from his jeans and hat, he walked over to the hotel desk, ringing the bell. The clerk emerged from the back, chewing what Gabe presumed was his dinner.

"Yes, sir, would you like a room?"

"No, I'm looking for Logan Granger." Gabe answered, watching the clerk open the guest register. "He might be registered."

The clerk ran the tip of a finger down the hotel register once then twice. "Sorry, there isn't a Granger checked in."

"He could have come in with the private stage earlier today," Gabe volunteered hoping Logan had at least once come in sometime during the day.

"Oh, yes, well, that party is in the dining room, waiting on fresh horses." The clerk pointed to a room that appeared to be empty. "Dinner begins service at six o'clock."

"Thank you." Gabe walked through the doorway scanning the tables as he entered. In a back corner sat a well-dressed family, looking completely out of place and reeking of money. He knew instantly they had to be the Manchesters. Looking further around the room, sitting at a table near the window was his old friend—Logan Granger.

***

Abby mentally checked off the few items on her list. In truth, she could have waited for Walter to bring them in a day or two, but since she was going, Abby didn't want to leave the post empty-handed. Placing the final item on the counter, Abby looked over the smaller pieces of material she could fashion into baby clothes or diapers. There were several pieces big and heavy enough she could make into window curtains once the weather turned colder.

"Miss Abby!" Charlie skipped out from the back room where Millie was helping Walter take inventory of their supplies. "Mama said she needs you."

He took her hand in his small one, pulling Abby with a child's excitement. "Hurry Miss Abby," he urged, pulling with both hands now.

"All right, Charlie." Abby laughed matching her steps to the stride of a seven-year-old.

"Mama, here's Miss Abby." Charlie announced his eyes bright with a secret, and his little chest puffed out. "I fetched her just like you asked."

"Goodness, Charlie, you'll pull Miss Abby's arm right off if you aren't careful." Walter chided his young son while trying to hide the smile on his face. "You did a fine job, son. Remember next time that you should treat girls and ladies gently. They ain't as tough as us men can be."

"Yes, Papa," Charlie replied looking up to Walter with nothing less than admiration.

"I'm fine, Walter. He's excited about helping out is

all." Abby smiled down at the dark-haired boy squashing the urge to ruffle the wild waves. "Now, what is so important that Charlie had to rush me in here?"

"Charlie, why don't you come out front with me?" Walter placed a firm hand on his son's shoulder, guiding him out of the storeroom. "I think there might be a peppermint if you help with me Miss Abby's purchases."

Abby giggled as Charlie ran to the counter, leaving his papa behind. "I surely do hope Gabe's as kind with our child as Walter is with Charlie. That boy really looks up to his father."

"Oh, don't let that kind-hearted man fool you. The boy gets punished when needed, so don't let Walter's show of softness lead you to believe otherwise," Millie said putting away the ledgers she'd been going over. "Extra chores always seem to do the trick when he's taken the wrong path."

"Hard work keeps young idle hands busy, that is true," Abby said, smoothing back her perfectly pinned hair. She paced around the back room taking in the small desk where Millie sat and the safe settled under a back table. Extra supplies were stacked on the shelves and floor to replenish any empty spots in the post.

"I've finished with my shopping." Abby sat in a chair in front of the desk. Her swollen belly perched in her lap, the baby grew restless. "Oh, he's busy in there today. Some days it feels like he's running in the fields while others are quiet as a Sunday morning in church."

"Abby" Millie looked as if she'd just swallowed a spoonful of tonic, "Walter feels it would be better for you to stay with us for a while. I sure would enjoy your company."

Stunned, Abby reached over giving her friend's hand a squeeze. "It's a kind offer Millie, but—"

"It would only be until Gabe comes back, is all," Millie said quietly, a faint look of hope in her eyes.

Abby ran a hand over the spot where the baby kicked in protest. "I can't, Millie. The mules and chickens need to be tended to. And there's much needing to be done before the baby comes. I appreciate Walter's concern and kind offer. As much as I would love being so close to you, I think I should stay in my own home."

Millie smiled, dismay skirting her eyes. "I told him you'd say that, but I did have to ask."

Abby stood slowly, letting the weight of the baby adjust inside her before stepping around the chair. "You and Walter are good friends, family really, and I thank you both. Gabe will be in agreement when I tell him of your generous offer,"

"Even if he chides you for not accepting," Millie teased looping an arm into the crux of Abby's elbow.

"Even then," Abby laughed. "Now, let's go see what your men are up to, shall we?"

They strolled to the front of the trading post where Charlie sat peering out the window on his knees. Millie joined her son, taking a hold of an arm and pulling him from his spying position.

"Papa told me to get inside when them two men rode up, Mama," Charlie whispered.

"It's okay, Charlie. Go to the back and play until I come to take you home," Millie told her son in that soothing voice of an experienced mother.

Abby watched as the boy trudged to the back, then turned her attention to window. From her point of view, Walter seemed stressed and a bit nervous the way his hands fidgeted with the edge of his vest. She couldn't get a clear look at the two other men. "What's going on, Millie?"

"I don't know. Walter's never sent him inside

before," Millie said just above a whisper.

Abby glanced out the window as one of the men gave Walter a shove. The situation outside wasn't a friendly one. It was one that alarmed and worried her.

Walter came up the step and into the trading post, the two men close behind. From the strained look on his face, Abby knew something was terribly wrong.

"Help yourself to whatever supplies you need," Walter offered, his gaze never wavering from Millie.

"Well, looky here, Billy. He's got hisself two women and one with child at that." The one in the gray shirt that hadn't seen a washtub in months spoke through a tobacco-stained grin. "We could have ourselves a party afore Jesse gets here."

"Shut up, Tom!" The one called Billy hissed the words, his black eyes darting around the room. "Where's the boy?"

"That boy can't hurt you," Abby said, the hackles on her neck prickling. Charlie may not be her son, but she wasn't about to let these two men scare her. Millie stood at the end of the counter blocking the path to her boy while Walter moved slowly behind her. Heat flushed through Abby with the knowledge Walter kept a rifle back there, but how long had it been since he'd actually used it? If he was going to use it she hoped his aim was true.

"No, but he could run out and get the law," Billy remarked, pushing his way past Millie and into the back room. "There's no back door and one window he'd have to climb up to get out of, Tom."

"Good, now which one of you fine-lookin' women is gonna cook us something to eat?" Tom quipped, his dull and lifeless eyes focused on Millie's bodice. "I ain't had good food for a long time."

"I will." Abby moved about gathering a few cans of

meat and several potatoes, maintaining eye contact with the filthy man. "Where do you suggest I cook?"

Walter stepped out from behind the counter and over to the potbelly stove. Grabbing several sticks of wood, he popped them into the fire pot. Millie was grabbing beans, bacon, and flour from the shelves, biting her bottom lip and avoiding eye contact with everyone.

While Millie mixed her ingredients into a pot, Abby peeled the potatoes. She guessed the men they were cooking for were members of the outlaws Gabe was looking for on the stage trail. Instead part of the Jesse Evans Gang loomed in Cook's Trading Post like nobody's business.

CHAPTER ELEVEN

"What are you doing here?" Gabe stood in front of Logan. "You should be back in Dodge with Rose."

"Nice to see you too," Logan replied motioning for Gabe to take a seat. "Pinkerton business. Manchester hired an agent to take them from Dodge City to Texas. I got the assignment once they rolled in on the train."

"Then you know—"

"That the Jesse Evans Gang is looking for them?" Logan smirked then downed the coffee sitting in front of him.

The tension in Gabe's shoulders lessened slightly with relief of that knowledge. At least Logan knew what he may be facing, and from the looks of the Manchesters they all would have their hands full.

"How's Abby?" Logan asked, filling the cup.

"Healthy and happy, I think. The baby is growing and so are Abby's moods." Gabe smiled, the warmth of love filling his heart. As much as the mood swings frustrated him, Gabe wouldn't change anything about Abby. She and the baby had become his reason for living a full life.

Logan chuckled, his eyes twinkling with fatherly knowledge. "It will get better after the baby comes. Until then do what she asks, don't ask questions, and you'll find a peaceful household."

Gabe nodded, "If only I'd had that advice before I told her not to leave the cabin."

"Ha, if she's anything like Rose she'll do the opposite!" Logan shook his head.

"Probably. She knows the danger though. I'm counting on her common sense to keep her safe." The image of Abby standing on the porch with tears in her eyes flooded his mind. He'd do whatever it took to see the smile back in them.

"Are they ready to leave?" Gabe nodded toward the family huddled in the back corner. "I didn't realize there were two children traveling as well. I hope they are well aware of the dangers along the trail."

"They are—at least as far as the stable. There's another stage coming through that they'll take to Texas and it won't be the one we'll be on." Logan looked up at the shadow cast over Gabe, his face etched in admiration.

Gabe smiled at the expression on his friend's face. There's only one person here in Silver City who could impress Logan. "Logan Granger, meet Deputy U.S. Marshal Bass Reeves."

Logan stood, extending a hand to the marshal. "Marshal, pleasure to finally meet you."

"Detective, I understand you're the best in the area." Bass shook Logan's hand then pulled out a chair, sitting between Gabe and Logan. "You come highly recommended by Mr. Pinkerton himself. Gabe and I can use another experienced gun. This gang is known to be violent with their victims."

Gabe watched the look on Logan's face go from

pride to worry to determination. Gabe knew how Bass did things even if he did question the marshal's motives from time-to-time. No doubt this would be no different.

"A telegram came earlier this morning from headquarters." Logan reached into his inside vest pocket, pulling out the folded telegram.

Bass took the missive, read it, then patted Gabe on the shoulder. "I'll be at the stable making sure the stage coach is ready to travel. Have that family ready to leave immediately."

Gabe watched Bass walk out the door as if on a leisurely Sunday stroll. "So, what's the plan, Logan?"

"Other than the real family staying here and us sitting like sitting ducks, I haven't the faintest. It's not my call. I was told to follow whatever orders Reeves gave." Logan replied, nudging Gabe in the chest. "The telegram carried a bit of news I wasn't counting on."

"I think it's time I had a long talk with a certain deputy U.S. marshal," Gabe pushed away from the table and with anger in check he walked out the door.

While Logan went about getting the Manchesters ready for departure, Gabe mounted his horse and rode over to the stable. If this plan was going to work he needed to know exactly what it was and if leaving his very pregnant wife to ride along with Bass was really justified...duty or not.

"Bass, mind telling me what is going on?" Gabe demanded, the reins grasped tightly in his fingers.

Bass was walking around the stagecoach inspecting the wheels and horses as they were hitched up. "Other than the fact that there's a report the Evans Gang has split up and my original plan is destroyed—"

"What do you mean, split up?" Spade's head jerked up when Gabe squeezed the reins in his hand. Looping the leather straps over a stall door, he flexed his fingers, releasing some of the tension. Gritting his teeth, Gabe moved close enough to Bass that he could feel him breathing. "Where the hell are they?"

"A couple of members headed toward Fred, while Jesse and the rest of the gang are spread out," Bass said softly.

Gabe reached out spinning Bass around to face him. "They are in Fred!"

"They were headed that way. Gabe, I have my scout out and—"

Gabe turned at the sound of children's giggles behind him. Standing in the stable doorway were the Manchesters dressed in their best travel clothes. Logan stood with the family, which was prepared to board the stagecoach.

"Sorry, folks, a change is necessary. We'll be traveling in one coach," Bass informed the passengers. "I know it's not what you expected, but you'll all be safer this way. I've already had your trunks loaded. Other than a few items for Mrs. Manchester and the children, your bags will be put in the rear boot.

Gabe helped the family get settled inside. Thoughts of the elevated danger surrounding his wife and unborn child at the center of his mind. He had to get to Fred before the members of the gang did.

"Keep inside the coach no matter what happens. The trail may be a bit rough in places, so you may bounce around some. Once we arrive in Fred—" Gabe told the family they'd get a hot meal and a place to rest while the horses were switched out. The children sat on opposite sides of the coach next to a parent holding their favorite toy, and he couldn't help but smile despite the lurking danger.

The coach rocked slightly as the driver and Logan stepped up into the driver's box. Bass brought up Spade and once Gabe mounted they all headed south out of town.

Please Lord, keep these fine people safe. Guide our hands in time of need. And keep my family safe from harm so that I might be with my wife and child through the years. Gabe prayed.

***

"Best damn meal I've had in a while," Billy said with his mouth full, giving Abby a pat on her bottom as she spooned more of the slop onto the outlaw's plate. "Where's your man anyways?"

Abby cringed with disgust at the stained toothy grin, "I would be much obliged if you kept your hands to yourself. And where my husband is, is no concern of yours. He's not here that's all you need to know," she spat, stomping back to the stove.

"You ain't got no call to lay your hands on the women. They done nothing but put food in your stomachs." Walter said from behind the counter, keeping his family tucked safely behind him. "We're God-fearin' people. Now take what you need and get on with your journey. I don't want no trouble here."

"Well, listen to that, will ya. The man does have a pair after all." Tom got up from the makeshift table of a board atop a barrel of pickles, pulling his gun from the holster. "Let's see if he can dance his way around this here floor, shall we?"

The sound of horses approaching drew Tom's attention from Walter to the window. As the outlaw holstered his pistol, Walter shooed Charlie and Millie into the backroom.

"Jesse's here," Tom announced, disappointment edging his craggy face. "Fun's over—for now." He sneered at Abby, damn near licking his chops at her. "Boss will be happy to see some purty faces."

The smile on the man's face sent a shiver up Abby's spine. Where was Gabe? He had to be coming by now. Unless…

Jesse Evans walked in the door with two other men trailing behind. "Boys, we have a situation. There's a Pinkerton and a marshal riding with that stagecoach. Taking it ain't gonna be as easy as I first thought. Didn't count on the dandy hiring a Pinkerton nor Reeves riding shotgun alongside."

"Hell, Jesse, we can take care of them two!" Billy said standing proud and tall with his chest puffed out like a rooster in a hen house. Tom shoved the last of his food into his mouth seeming oblivious to the other men.

"Well, now, Billy, that may be true. The problem here is that Reeves is riding with them. And in these parts the Creek is his family." Jesse scoured the trading post, his gaze landing on Abby's face then skirted down to her belly where the baby was kicking up a storm.

"Sorry, ma'am, I hope my boys have been treating you kindly," Jesse said, tipping his hat. "Sometimes I do wonder where their manners have gone."

Abby snorted, her spine ridged and the pot of ham and beans still in her hand. "They could use some manners that's for sure. Their mamas would be ashamed of them!"

Billy took two steps toward her, his gun drawn, mouth turned down and eyes as cold as a winter's night. Jesse stuck out his arm, blocking any further advance.

"You are a spirited one at that. The lady is right, Billy, and you know it." Jesse waved his man off toward the window his tone controlled offering no room of discussion. "Now go sit down and keep watch out that window. We will wait here for the rest of the boys to bring that stage and its riches to us."

Tom looked up from his empty plate as if realizing

for the first time their leader was there. "Where's the rest of the boys?"

"Watching the trail and hoping to get a clear shot at the lawmen before the stage arrives," Jesse answered, surveying the room. It was at that time Charlie could be heard arguing with Millie in the back.

"Mama, I gotta pee," the boy exclaimed as he ran out and straight into the leg of Jesse Evans.

"Whoa there, little man." Jesse gabbed Charlie's arm, stopping him as he tried to dodge around the gunman's leg.

"Get. Your. Hand. Off. My. Boy." Walter ordered, the once hidden rifle now pointed at Evans.

Before Walter could take aim and pull the trigger, a shot exploded around them. "Argh!" Walter grunted then dropped the rifle as he slumped to the floor, blood seeping from his shoulder. Millie screamed and ran to his side, trying to stop the bleeding as she ripped a strip of cloth from the bottom of her skirt and sniffed back the tears.

"It's only a small wound, ma'am, but I can't have your man thinking he's something he's not." Jesse smiled at Charlie, ruffling the boy's hair. "Still have to pee, boy?"

"N-n-n-no," Charlie whimpered, the front of his britches wet.

Abby walked over to Charlie, taking his hand in hers. "Come with me, Charlie," she said as calmly as she could. She looked directly into Evans' eyes daring him to challenge her. When none came, she took the boy into the back room. "Let's get you into fresh pants, won't that feel better?"

"Yes, Miss Abby. Is Papa gonna die?" Charlie asked, throat working as he swallowed back the fear in his words.

"Your mama's lookin' after him," Abby said, pulling a pair of pants off the shelf, holding them up to his waist. "Now these look like they'll fit."

Helping the young boy out of his soiled pants, Abby kept an eye on the doorway. "Shh," she whispered putting a finger up to her lips. "Charlie, you are such a brave boy. How would you like to be a deputy just for today?"

Charlie's fallen face brightened. "Like Gabe?"

"Yes, like Gabe." Abby glanced out the doorway again, making sure their captors weren't paying her any attention. She hurried over to the window, motioning for Charlie to come to her. "Now, listen very carefully. I want you to crawl out of the window. Go straight over to our place and get on one of the mules. Ride as fast as you can to your house and find a somewhere to hide where no one will find you. Do you understand, Charlie?"

Charlie nodded, then climbed out the window with Abby's help. Once she saw him run along the tree line in the direction of her cabin, she silently closed the window.

"You get some rest now, Charlie. I'll come wake you when supper's ready," Abby called out loud enough to be heard by the outlaws in the front. She ran her hands down the front of the apron, took a deep breath, and walked out to the front of the trading post.

Please Lord, guide Charlie safely to the house where he can hide. And bring Gabe here as soon as you can.

***

Gabe rode along the trail beside the coach. Logan sat next to the driver with a shotgun draped over his knee, while Bass kept watch on the east side of the trail. So far the ride had been uneventful, and Gabe was surprised by the lack of complaints from the passengers. It was a hot and dusty day. The faint call of a bird came from somewhere on the plains. A light wind out of the south hit Gabe in the face, causing him to pull the brim of his hat over his eyes.

Bass spurred his horse up to the driver, said something, and the coach came to a rolling stop. He glanced quickly over at Gabe then rode off toward the lone rider about a half-mile to the east.

"Why have we stopped?" Manchester demanded, sticking his head out the window.

"I'm not sure, sir. I'll ask the driver." Gabe rode up next to the driver's box.

"What's going on?" Gabe flexed his fingers around the reins, an empty dark hole widening in the pit of stomach. "It's not safe for us to be sitting out in the open like this while he goes off for a social visit with whoever that rider is."

"Reeves said to stop, give the horses a rest and the Manchesters a chance to stretch their legs." Logan shrugged. "You know better than anyone the man does strange things, but he is always successful, isn't he, Gabe?"

Gabe grunted, reluctantly dismounted, then swung the coach door open. "Everything's okay folks. Now would be a good time to get up and move a bit, but stay out of the brush and near the stage. It's hot and the rattlers could be cooling under a rock or in brush."

"My daddy's a doctor, mister," the little Manchester boy said with a snip in his tiny voice. "Ain't no rattler gonna hurt me."

"Well, then, that's a good thing to know you are a brave boy." Gabe nodded then walked Spade to the back of the stagecoach to keep an eye on Bass. Whoever was out there he'd found it important enough to stop their progress. They couldn't be far from Fred now. Gabe guessed maybe another ten miles or so and he'd be home holding Abby in his arms.

The longing he felt for her surprised him every time he thought of her. He needed to feel the warmth of her body. To feel their baby move within the layers of her swollen belly. Gabe couldn't wait to count each little toe and finger when the time came. To share her pain in childbirth as best he could. Both of them molding their son into a fine young man.

Sure, at first he didn't know how to handle the fact that he, of all people, was going to be a father. Taking an older woman with no children for a bride that he'd hoped to be barren was one thing, but a child? A child had been an entity far from his plans. He wasn't sure when the deck of cards had been changed and stacked with fatherhood.

After he'd come to his senses he knew having both Abby and the baby gave him a second chance to live a life he'd dreamed of as a young man. All he wanted was to see Abby's smiling face and breath the scent of lavender on her soft skin.

But he had to get home first and the sooner the better. Stopping wasn't going to accomplish that.

Gabe looked up at the sound of hoofbeats across the hard land to see Bass heading back to the stagecoach. Walking over to the side of the coach, Gabe held the door open.

"Okay, folks, looks like we'll be on our way. Please get on board." Gabe watched the little ones, followed by Mrs. Manchester, climb up into the coach. Dr. Manchester paused for a moment, scowled, then nodded as he stepped up into the stage.

Gabe closed the door, making sure it was secure. If they needed to hightail it out of there the last thing they needed was for that door to swing open and someone to fall out. Mounting Spade, he rode out to meet Bass.

"Mind telling me what that was all about?" Gabe asked, reining to a stop next to Bass.

"That was one of my scouts. He found several of the Evans gang ready to ambush us a few miles up. Fortunately, they won't be doing much harm now." Bass grinned, as he let his horse catch its breath.

"Great, that means we should have a clear path all the way to Fred. Then tomorrow this family can move on to Texas." Every muscle in Gabe's body relaxed all at once. A giddy feeling, like a young man going on his first hunt, crept into him.

Bass moved in next to Gabe close enough that all he'd have to do was reach out and grab Gabe's holstered gun. Gabe had Spade take a side step away from Bass, giving himself room to move.

"Bass, you know better than to crowd a man and his gun. What aren't you telling me?"

"There's one more thing. They found little Charlie Cook on one of your mules about a mile from your place. The boy said he was a deputy just like Marshal Hawkins. The boy said his pa was shot, and Miss Abby helped him out the window, telling him to go home and find a place to hide until someone came for him." Bass's words were quiet and said with intention. "He's going back to keep an eye on the post. There's a brave watching over Charlie at the Cook's place."

"The hell you say! I'm leaving without you, Bass. *Now!*" Gabe turned Spade's head then took off at a gallop straight for Fred. And Abby.

No matter to Gabe if Deputy U.S. Marshal Bass Reeves shouted for him or not. His words were lost. Gabe rode the black quarter horse at a run. Giving the horse its head it felt the urgency in Gabe's body and stretched out at a full gallop.

Visions of Walter Cook lying dead on the floor of the trading post with Millie sobbing over him and Abby trying to calm her flooded his mind. Then there was Abby huddled with Millie in a corner of the trading post frightened out of their wits. One of Abby being mishandled by one of the outlaws spurred the surge of blood in his veins.

"Yaw!" Gabe yelled, slapping Spade on the shoulders with the reins.

I'll kill the bastards if they touch her!

CHAPTER TWELVE

"How's Walter?" Abby knelt next to Millie, handing her a clean cloth to hold over the bullet wound. "Keep it as clean as you can, Millie."

"I think the bleeding has stopped, but he hasn't come to again." Millie's smile quivered with false bravery. Her unconscious husband's head lay cradled in her lap. "Where's Charlie?"

"I sent him home," Abby whispered, patting her friend on an arm. Standing, she moved around to the front of the counter leaving the Cooks in what Abby felt had to be a relatively safe place. Sooner or later one of the outlaws would be asking about the boy, hopefully not before help arrived. But it was getting late. The sun would begin to set soon and the chances of the stage arriving before the darkness came was slight.

Jesse Evans stood looking out the window, his head moving from side to side. "That stage should be here before long. Once the passengers get inside we'll tie everyone up and leave with the stage and everything in it. Since there's not a town for miles, no reason to leave these fine people with a way to get help."

"Why leave anyone alive, Jesse? They're all witnesses," Tom pointed out, spitting a stream of tobacco into the spittoon on the floor. "We could take the women for a bit of fun and—"

"Shut up, Tom! We ain't got time for you to put your seed into no woman," Billy squawked from his perch near the stove. Of the three outlaws, he seemed to be the orneriest.

"Hell, Billy. It's been a while. I need some relief," Tom whined, pushing away from the table.

"Then get your ass outside in the outhouse for a piece and take care of your needs," Jesse ordered. "I'll not put up with you talkin' filth around these respectable ladies."

Grumbling, Tom stepped outside the door and headed toward the stable where a small outhouse stood.

"Sorry, ladies," Jesse smirked, looking a tad less than sincere. "Tom is a Chapter short of a dime store novel sometimes. He needs to take some pressure off his pickle, then he'll be right as rain."

"That's not all he needs," Abby suggested, glaring at the two men left in the post. "You all need a good dose of manners and rehabilitation time in the local jailhouse!"

Jesse grabbed her by the arm. Instinctively, she swung out leaving a bright red mark across his cheek. Her heart skipped a beat, the blow doing little to deter the man's hold on her.

"Keep your hands off of me." Abby struggled to pull out of the vice grip of fingers. "You're hurting me."

Jesse sneered, his eyes bright and deadly. "Good, then maybe you'll do as I say from now on."

"You've got another thing coming if you believe that for one minute," Abby bit back, her jaw tightly set.

"We'll see about that. Let's see what you'll do to

protect a child, shall we?" Jesse smirked, the lines in his face hard with determination. "Billy, go in the back and get the boy!"

Billy nodded then marched into the back of the trading post "The boy's gone!" he yelled, standing in the doorway with a pillow and blanket in his hands.

"Gone? How—" Jesse jerked on Abby's arm almost pulling it from its socket. "Where is the boy?"

Abby grinned at him through the pain his tightening grip delivered. "Far from you reaching him!"

Her chest clinched with fear diminishing the bravado of a moment ago. What if Charlie was hanging around outside? The outlaws would surely find him and probably use him against them.

"Damn woman! Billy, go fetch Tom. Then the two of you go looking for the kid. Start in the barn, a boy that young has to be hiding nearby," Jesse demanded, forcing Abby down in a chair.

"Do you really think they'll find Charlie?" Millie asked from behind the counter.

"For your sake and that of your husband's, my men damn well better find the brat," Jesse hissed between clinched teeth. His eyes were cold and full of a darkness that made Abby shiver. Would he really hurt an innocent child just to prove a point?

Millie gasped her eyes full of fright. "No-o-o-o!"

"Don't worry, Millie, I'm sure those two idiots won't be able to find a clever seven-year-old boy who knows this area like the back of his hand," Abby offered, her gaze darting back to Jesse.

He seemed nervous, worried as far as Abby could tell by the way he shifted about from one leg to another. Maybe he believed Charlie had gotten away. The boy better have done as she told him and hightailed it home to hide. If not she'd never forgive herself if something happened to Charlie.

"You'll hold your tongue, woman!" Jesse demanded from his station at the window. "What is taking them so long? They should have found him by now."

Jesse yanked Abby out of the chair, pointing his gun at Millie. "You try anything and this baby won't live any longer than its mother."

Abby tried to yank her arm away, but the more she struggled the tighter his grip became. She was practically dragged out the door and across the porch by an elbow. Her heart hammered in her bosom as they rounded the corner of the post. Spade stood among the team of horses meant for the next stage.

Dear God, he's back!

Jesse yanked her to an abrupt stop. There in the corral, plain as day, Tom and Billy were tied to a post, limp as wet rags. Their heads hanging off to the side, eyes closed, and gags in their mouths.

Abby looked at Jesse, a smile on her face. "My husband is home."

"Get your hands off my wife!" Gabe yelled from the hayloft, the buffalo rifle Walter kept hidden there resting against his shoulder. "You heard me. Let go of my wife!" Gabe fired a warning shot that buzzed past the outlaws.

"Gabe!" Abby let out a scream of surprise. Gabe knew with all his heart no matter how brave she acted she had to be scared as a rabbit.

"The next one will be between your eyes," Gabe warned, reloading the rifle.

"Will you risk her life as well as the baby's?" Evans held a gun to Abby's head.

Abby squared her shoulders, her hand clenching and unclenching. "Don't listen to him, Gabe. He won't hurt me!"

"Shut up, woman." Evans snarled, grabbing her cheeks and pinching her mouth shut. "You have no idea what I'm capable of doing. And neither does your man."

Gabe felt his body tremble with rage. He had to find a way to distract Evans. Get his attention away from Abby for a moment, that's all he'd need to get a clear shot.

"You really think I'll miss and give you a chance to pull that trigger?" Gabe called out, hoping Evans would nibble at a little distraction bait.

"I can hear it in your voice. You're scared." Evans looked around quickly, moving closer to the horses. "Scared I'm gonna hurt your woman."

All Gabe would have to do was whistle. Spade would breach the fence, taking the herd and Evans with him. He wasn't willing to take the chance of Abby and the baby getting caught among the runaway horses though.

"What do you want, Evans?" Gabe crouched down, hoping to get a better angle to take a shot.

"You to come out in the open and face me like a man for starters," Evans called out, gathering Abby in his arms. Her back against Evans' chest was a shield against any gunfire.

"Never took you to be the kind to hide behind the skirts of a woman, Evans." Gabe moved to his left and climbed down from the hayloft and toward the back of the barn.

"I'm not. But I'd also like to know who is shooting at me!" Evans cocked his head to one side, taking a few steps backward. "And who the man is willing to put his lovely wife and unborn child in danger."

Gabe slipped out the back door of the barn, stealing round the south end along the tree line. If he could reach the outhouse he might get a clear shot at Evans.

"Marshal Hawkins at your service," Gabe yelled, stepping out from a cluster of trees and tall brush.

"Ya know who you're dealing with, Hawkins?" Evans laughed, a slow smile of confidence creeping across his face.

Gabe moved in behind the outhouse and assessed his vantage point. He'd been right. From here he could get a clear shot without endangering Abby—as long as Evans didn't change position that is.

"I would guess Jesse Evans, leader of 'The Boys.' And since the rest of your little gang are all being held as prisoners in one way or another, you are left here on your own." Gabe lifted the rifle, getting Evans in his sight.

"My men are smarter than that!" Evans shouted, his easy confidence dwindling away.

"As smart as the two tied up in the corral?" Gabe baited again. "That's not very smart, is it?"

Evans backed up toward the trading post, dragging Abby along with him. An arm was tight around her neck and shoulders while the gun in his hand roamed from side to side slowly.

"You're a coward, marshal. Come out and face me like a man," Evans challenged.

"Let my wife go and I'll show myself. Until then I'd watch my back if I were you," Gabe warned. "I won't give you another chance to give up."

Evans swung around, his arm loosening around Abby.

"Drop, Abby!" Gabe yelled then stepped out from behind the out building. Abby jumped out of Evans' grasp, falling hard on her side on the ground.

BOOM!

Gabe fired, winging Evans in his shooting arm. Evans rolled, reached for his fallen firearm. The gun in his hand he pulled the trigger, barely missing Abby but catching Gabe in the leg. Gabe collapsed, his gun still in his hand, and shot back hitting the outlaw in the shoulder.

The sound of horses thundered into Fred. The last thing Gabe remembered seeing was a blur of white standing between Abby and Evans.

Several hours later Abby woke from what could only be described as a nightmare. Gunfire. Outlaws. Gabe being shot. And her falling to the ground on her side.

"My baby!" Panic raced through her heart and soul, remembering her hard fall to the ground as shots were fired.

"Ohhh," she mewed in relief, placing a hand over her belly where the baby moved, letting her know he was still there.

"Stay quiet, Abby," Gabe coaxed, his hand giving hers a light squeeze. "Doc says you need bedrest for a few days."

"You, you were shot!" Abby whispered, a tear slipping out of her eye.

"It was nothing compared to thinking you and the baby were hurt." Gabe leaned in, kissing her on the forehead, brushing several wisps of hair back. "Once the rush left my body and I knew you were safe, I let go. Logan and Bass got you into bed, while Dr. Manchester treated my leg. The bullet went clear through and missed the bone and artery."

"Logan? Logan is here?" The words pitched high

enough for the angels to hear.

"Logan was the Pinkerton assigned to escort the Manchesters from Dodge to Texas. As it turns out, Douglas Manchester is a doctor who has decided to stay in Fred rather than travel further south. He said he wants to be where he's needed the most. Evidently he believes it's right here." Gabe sat in a chair next to her, his left leg propped up on another.

"So, we have a doctor now for when the baby comes?" Abby's eyes widened in delight. "That's wonderful. Are you sure he's staying though?"

"I sure am. And I've given specific orders that you are to rest." Dr. Manchester towered over her, his face gentle and kind with a twinkle in his eye.

Abby took an instant liking to the man. He had an easygoing manner even as he stood at the end of her bed, assessing her with his gaze.

"By my examination and after a long talk with your husband, I believe you may have the baby a little earlier than you thought," Dr. Manchester informed her, his grin spreading across his face.

"No, the babe's not due for three months," Abby insisted, fear exploding through her mind. "Is the baby okay?"

"Yes Abby, the doctor said the baby is fine despite the ordeal you've gone through the past few days," Gabe assured, his face worn from worry and pain.

Dr. Manchester picked up her wrist, checking her pulse. "Mrs. Hawkins, you have miscalculated your pregnancy by a few weeks. And given what you've experienced, if the baby comes early—"

"Comes early? Why would the baby come early?" Abby bit her lower lip, and took a few deep breaths to calm herself.

"He won't if you do exactly as the doc here says.

No more laundry or lifting even a pound of flour, Abby," Gabe ordered gently.

Dr. Manchester laughed. "That may be a bit extreme, Mr. Hawkins. I'm not suggesting the baby isn't healthy. On the contrary, it is very active and doesn't appear to be in any distress. Babies come when they are ready to take on the world; yours will be no different. I only want you to stay in bed for a week. Give your mind and body time to heal." Dr. Manchester patted her on the hand, winked, then left the room.

Relief surged through Abby. She looked over at Gabe, catching a glimmer of tears in his eyes.

"I'll do whatever I need to for our baby…and my husband," she promised.

Gabe broke down sobbing, tears running down over his face. "I'm so sorry, Abby. I put both you and the baby in danger by leaving. I broke my promise to always protect you. My parents were right. I'm broken as a man."

"No, Gabe. You did what you needed to do as a lawman," Abby reminded him.

"But I'm a broken man, Abby. Don't you see that?"

"What I see is a man I love beyond life itself. Gabe, we are all broken until we find the right pieces to make us whole again." Abby slowly moved his hand over to her belly, lacing her fingers with his as their baby squirmed under the protection of his mama and papa.

EPILOGUE

"How does it feel to finally have that little one in your arms, Abby?" Millie asked as she set a pot of stewed meat on the stove.

"Do I really have to explain that to you, Millie? You know what a blessing the little one has been." Abby looked down at her baby sleeping peacefully against her breast, the round little face free of worry.

"We are thankful for both you and Walter for being here," Gabe said, bringing in a bucket of milk with Charlie handling the basket of eggs with experience. "I couldn't have handled listening to Abby screaming in pain if not for Walter taking me out behind the barn to cut more wood. I think we'll have more than enough for the winter months and any repairs that may need to be done."

Walter reached out, slapping Gabe on the shoulder. "If not for you, Gabe, some of us might not be here today. It could have been just you and Charlie."

"Well, let's not dwell on that right now, Walter. I think it's time for us to go home and tend to our own family." Millie took her husband's arm and guided him out the door. "If you need anything, Abby, send Gabe and I'll be right down."

"I will," Abby grinned, waving as their neighbors boarded their wagon and headed east down the road.

"You aren't disappointed are you, Gabe?" Abby asked, moving slightly as the babe sleepily suckled milk.

Gabe sat next to her, his eyes bright with moisture. "Disappointed? Why in the world would I be disappointed, Abby? Our baby is healthy. Dr. Manchester said there'll be no ill effects from the fall you took. That both you and baby are doing well."

"Yes, I know, but you wanted..." Abby reached out for her husband, her lifeline to everything.

"A boy," Gabe answered, no trace of disappointment in his eyes. "I got something more precious. Little Angela Marie Hawkins will be every bit like her mother. She'll be a fine big sister to keep her little brother in line."

Abby laughed, joy filling her heart. "So you want to have another baby?"

Gabe drew her and their darling little girl into his arms. "I want as many babies as God is willing to give us."

THE END

BONUS EXCERPT

THE RELUCTANT BRIDE

PROLOGUE

Southcentral Wisconsin
Late April, 1877

"Have you lost your senses?" Miss Roseanne Duncan looked over the advertisement for a mail order bride, the paper rattling in her hand. "I can't become a mail order bride. Besides, he's expecting you."

"Doesn't matter," Abigail Johnson replied, continuing to sort through the tub of fresh vegetables. "This is your best chance to survive and you know it."

A sick feeling went through her at Abby's blunt words, memories of the mistress falling to her death, the master at the top of the stairs assailed her. She shuddered. The memorial was set for today. It was only a matter of time until... No she couldn't think it. A chance to get away...could she really take it? Rose read over the advertisement flier again. "Abby, this looks more like a wanted poster than a man in search of a wife."

"Granted, it shows he is a bit creative, and educated by the way it's worded." Abigail peeked over the top of the page, then returned to picking out the best of the potatoes.

Rose was still stunned by Abby's plan to become a mail order bride. "Yes, I'll give him that much at least he's literate. Why would you feel the need to answer something like this in the first place?" Rose had heard dubious stories of mail order brides and very few of them ended well. "You're a wonderful cook and passionate woman, any local man would be lucky to have you. You don't need to answer an advertisement from a Wild West gentleman, if he is one, that you don't know and move off to who knows where."

"Maybe I wanted to grab my last chance for adventure," she said with a grin.

Rose felt bad not wanting to hurt her feelings. "Oh, I didn't mean to…"

"Don't you worry about it. I'll take the next one who suits my fancy. This is exactly what you need after what happened. Rose, what have you got to lose?" Abigail whispered, scrubbing the dirt from the potatoes for supper that night. "You need to leave this house as soon as you can. They'll be burying the lady in a few days, but people are already talking. It's no secret she'd become ill, Rose. But sickness didn't break her neck and everybody's talking about it. Even Mrs. Griswold's family has grown suspicious."

"I've heard the rumors, but we both know the truth. Mrs. Griswold wasn't ill enough to fall to the bottom of the staircase on her own Abby. I know what I saw." Rose grabbed her friend's hand and squeezed it lightly. "He knows I saw him do it."

"All the more reason to get out of town before someone questions you." Abigail ceased her scrubbing, her brow furrowed she looked Rose square in the face. "Have you considered the consequences of that testimony if her family presses forward with an investigation? You know he could make it look like you're the one who 'helped' his wife down the stairs that night. He'll make them believe you were in love with him, throwing yourself at him at every opportunity to lure him from his poor sickly wife."

Rose recoiled from the thought of that snide monster touching her. "No one will believe that story. They can't, it's not true." Even as she said it she knew it wasn't true. She was a mere servant and an impoverished one at that. He was wealthy. No one would believe her if it came to her word against his. It was why she hadn't gone to the law even though it pricked her conscience to keep silent. It just plain went against her personal code of justice to let him go unpunished. The horrific scene played across her mind again.

Rose had been starting her morning duties when she heard them arguing at the top of the stairs. Mrs. Griswold didn't want to go down for an early breakfast that day; she wanted to go back to her room. Mr. Griswold kept insisting she make an appearance so the staff wouldn't think she was sickly. Rose had often wondered if the source of the wasting sickness had come from the master's own hand. All he'd have to do was slip something into her tea. She shuddered knowing it was too late to save her mistress now.

That morning, they'd continued to argue and then came the scream. The horrible sound of a body tumbling down the stairs, and Mr. Griswold standing at the top of the landing with smug indifference on his face. When he turned and saw her, the look in his eyes when they locked on hers was dark, dead and cold as a winter's frigid night, promising retribution if she said anything. She'd shivered and dashed back up the servant's staircase, hiding in her room until the other maids began to move about the house. Then a scream rang out from the scullery maid and Rose knew the mistress had been found.

So far there hadn't been any question as to how Mrs. Griswold came to be at the bottom of the staircase. Mr. Griswold told the doctor and police officers that she'd tripped over a rug at the top of the landing. She hadn't had a lantern with her so she could see in the hallway. And since Mr. Griswold was a wealthy man, his explanation had gone unchallenged. Even so, Mrs. Griswold's family threatened to hire an investigator for all the good that would do Mrs. Griswold now.

Rose chased the fresh memory from her mind and looked over the advertisement again. Abby was right, she had no other choice but to run. But this, could she even contemplate being a mail order bride, tying herself to a man she didn't even know? According to the paper, a man named Logan Granger was looking for a mail order bride to help manage his household and his six-year-old daughter. It indicated he was a widower of means, healthy, and respected at the age of thirty. Mr. Granger wrote that he lived in a stylish house in the frontier town of Dodge City, Kansas. Far from Mr. Griswold's reach she thought taking heart. There was no mention of wifely duties, just the household and the child. Mr. Logan Granger basically wanted a housekeeper and nanny for the price of marriage and a home.

But, Kansas? Could she move so far away just to escape the fury of Atticus Griswold, who would certainly become her former employer before long and probable accuser? How could she be sure she wasn't walking into something far worse than she'd be leaving? What could be worse than the gallows, she thought wryly as her conscience smote her. Marrying someone she didn't love. So who needed love?

Looking at the ad it seemed love wasn't one of the requirements. Besides when she got there if they didn't suit she could cry off. She was afraid her heart wouldn't allow her to marry a man she didn't at least feel affection for. Could she make an exception for one who made no mention of love? And then there was Dodge City itself. She'd read the papers. Dodge City had a reputation for being a wild town brimming with gamblers, gunfighters, and saloon girls of the night.

"Abby, even if it were possible there's no reason for this man to even want me. I'm a housemaid with no experience at taking care of a little girl. Not to mention, he sounds like he's a pretty important man in his town. What would he want with a housemaid for a bride who doesn't even know how to cook?" Rose placed the paper on the counter top, her heart heavy with sadness. She had no right to think a man like the one Mr. Granger sounded like would actually want a servant for a wife. Then again, maybe that's exactly all he wanted. After all, he did indicate he was looking for someone to manage his household and look after his little girl, nothing more. Would that mean she'd have her own bedroom, or would she have to share a room with Mr. Granger, her prospective husband?

"You can follow a recipe, can't you?" Abigail shot her a side glance, the corner of her mouth moving into a small smile. "What if he didn't care what you did for a living?"

"And how would you know that? This man doesn't

want a runaway witness for a bride. He'll want someone to match his stature. Someone substantial who comes with the full knowledge of how a household runs." Rose took the paper between her fingers, giving it one last look over before tossing it into the day's waste.

"And you don't have that knowledge?" Abigail wiped her hands on her apron, then reached into her pocket. "I don't know, but there's only one way to find out." She offered Rose an envelope with Abigail's name and address scrolled across it. "He wants me and I'm only a cook and much older than he is. So obviously he isn't fussy. Why wouldn't he want a pretty young wife instead of a matronly one?"

"Abby, what have you done?" Rose took the envelope, pulling out a piece of parchment folded neatly into thirds. Tucked into the folds of the letter was a ticket for the next train to Kansas City, where she'd then switch trains and continue to travel the rest of the way to Dodge City.

"Giving my dear friend the chance to live, if she'll take it."

CHAPTER ONE

Dodge City, Kansas
Early May, 1877

Logan Granger tugged at his vest once again. What a fool hair-brained idea it was to advertise for a bride and expect her to come to Dodge City of all places, but he was between a rock and a hard place. If not for Lilly, he wouldn't have done it. But Dodge was no place for a six-year-old girl to be running around without supervision. He couldn't watch her and do his job without having to worry where she was all the time. It wasn't fair to keep her locked in a room at the Lady Gay either. She needed room to run and play, and grow into a fine young woman like her momma.

Logan pulled the watch from the vest pocket. His father had given him the keepsake the day Logan had graduated from Harvard law school. He smiled remembering that day. Pop had been so proud of him. All Logan had to do was find a respectable law firm to establish himself in, then find a girl from a good family to marry and settle down. He'd done it all; he'd taken up with the law firm of Winston & Blodgett in Chicago in 1870, after he married Katie Blanchard of Boston, became a father to Lilly the following year, and then lost Katie to scarlet fever somewhere within five years of their marriage—the exact date escaped him. He wanted to find a way to escape the pain of losing her, and soon realized what he'd really been looking for was a way to join her.

So he resigned from the firm and went to work undercover for the Pinkerton Detective Agency in Chicago. He'd worked with the detective agency through the law firm for a few years on various court cases he'd taken on. Many of his cases had him working especially hand-in-hand with Mr. Pinkerton himself, and Logan found a real camaraderie with the man every outlaw feared. His work gave him a new-found purpose and he soon realized Lilly needed her daddy more than Logan needed to join Katie. It was only then that he realized the error of his ways. He might need the oblivion of danger to make himself feel whole again but Lilly's needs had to come first. Pushing the sadness aside, Logan flipped the gold inscribed cover closed and pushed the watch back into his waistcoat.

"Sure hope you know what you're doing bringing that woman here, Logan." Marshal Dane Jones stood next to Logan, rocking back on his heels. The marshal had recently sent four women on the last wagon train from the fort to Santa Fe. Chaperoned by Nellie Ward, Jones felt it was in the young women's best interests to find husbands to look after them. Logan smiled, he'd heard the Widow Markham had married before she even left town.

"So do I, Marshal. After all, I got the notion from you." Logan looked up and down the tracks avoiding making eye contact with the marshal. "I didn't see any other way. Lilly's gonna be a young lady before I know it, and she needs a mature woman to guide her along the right path."

"I know a few ladies in town more than willing to be your wife, you didn't need to send for a store bought one." Jones chuckled, slapping Logan on the back.

Logan looked at the marshal shaking his head. "I'm particular, Marshal. I don't need that kind of distraction in my line of work."

"How particular can it be to find a wife? As long as she's willing to lay with you, cook your meals, and wash your clothes what is she there for?" The marshal winked, then chuckled again.

"You never cease to astound me, Marshal. How about a little something called companionship, trust, honor? Bed doesn't come into the equation." No, he couldn't even contemplate letting a woman get that close to his heart again. To make sure of it, he'd hand picked the right candidate. "I've got a little girl to think of. Taking this wife to bed is not what I'm looking for." Logan shuffled his feet, then took his hat off slapping the dust off the brim before settling it back over his thick black hair. "Abigail Johnson will be my wife in name only. She's older, respectable, and well versed in the running of a household, and she'll be the perfect woman to properly guide Lilly along."

"I can see where Lilly would be of a concern to you, Logan. Are you sure this woman won't run off with the first slick gambler she meets? I've got enough trouble in this town without you bringing this city woman in to add to it."

"Of that I'm sure, Dane. Miss Johnson will be the perfect 'mature' woman to take care of Lilly should anything happen to me."

"I see." Marshall Jones tucked his thumbs into his gun belt, then turned looking Logan in the face. "Any leads on that cattle rustling business yet?"

"Nothing solid, or worth mentioning." Logan dragged his gaze across the street, watching the upstanding citizens of Dodge come and go from the stores lining Front Street. Dodge City was starting to grow into a true metropolis of more than drovers and gamblers. Families were settling just outside of town farming the land and raising dairy cows. There were more women and children walking the streets every day. The train did its share to bring them from Boston to the wild west. It amazed him that more stayed then left when things got a bit tough on them. It took true grit to make a home in the untamed west.

"Well, I'll leave you to it. Preacher Samuels sent me over to let you know he'll be in the Long Branch awaitin'. Shouldn't be too long now." Marshal Jones turned, leaving Logan to mull over his upcoming nuptials.

Any moment now his bride would be arriving. She'd step off the Santa Fe, walk across the street and straight into the Long Branch to get married. No courtship. No getting to know each other. No time to fall in love. It was better that way.

According to the letter from Abigail Johnson of

Wisconsin, she was of an age past the time of bearing a child, and that suited Logan just fine. She implied she'd always longed for a daughter to love and guide through her young years. Miss Johnson also indicated she managed the kitchen of a rather large estate for several years, but wanted to seek out on an adventure before she walked into her later years. In short she sounded perfect.

Miss Johnson hadn't sent a photograph, stating it didn't matter what either of them looked like since this was to be a marriage of convenience and in name only, which suited him just fine. She was willing to share his name, help raise Lilly, make his meals, and any other household duties, but she refused to share his bed. She'd wrote if that was accommodating to him, she gladly accepted his terms and proposal of marriage.

Logan was definitely accommodating to those terms; he'd set them after all. He'd had the extra room next to Lilly's prepared for his "wife" and at the opposite end of the hall from him. That way they'd barely have to cross paths in the bedroom area if they didn't want to. He aimed to have his daughter safely under the protection and guidance, if not love, of Miss Johnson should something happen to him during his cattle rustling investigation.

When he'd accepted the undercover assignment to Dodge City, he'd not thought of Lilly's future nor what would happen to his young daughter if he were killed. That had been six months ago. It didn't take him long to realize that Dodge wasn't the place for motherless children, even though several families had settled in the area, and he couldn't bear to send her to the family ranch in northern Montana. Dodge was still the stomping ground of every cowpoke, gambler and gunfighter passing through town.

It had taken some time, but once Logan had secured

his place as barkeep at the Lady Gay, he'd saved enough money to add to his Chicago bank accounts; he got Lilly and him out of the Dodge House and into a home of their own. The sparsely furnished, two-story sat on the north edge of town, but lacked a woman's touch. His new wife would soon set that right. He missed the smell of a home cooked meal coming from the kitchen and sitting down to eat like a family without half the town for company. He felt certain Miss Johnson would provide that for Lilly.

The train whistle blared as it roared into town, chasing away Logan's thoughts of the warm and welcoming home he admitted to be missing.

Logan adjusted his hat and tie. "Looks like my bride has arrived right on time."

Rose Duncan clenched the letter tightly in her hand. Going over in her mind the past few days of how her life was in a flux of change, she gazed up at the train she was about to finish her escape in. She was still in disbelief that she'd taken Abby up on her outrageous suggestion. Part of her felt freer than she had in…well, forever. She could do this. Manage this man's household and daughter. She loved children and they usually took to her. She felt bad that she'd done Abby out of this adventure, but Abby assured her she'd find a more suitable, older man to marry as there seemed to be plenty of them available out west.

After a brief stop in Kansas City where she switched trains, Rose glanced over her shoulder then stepped up into a train for the last time, making a wish for luck. Whatever came, she knew she'd never see Wisconsin again. She'd left everything behind in her small room on the third floor of her former employer's house. In haste, she had put on the only clean dress and undergarments she had before taking the stage to Chicago for what felt like months ago. Abigail insisted she travel without bags so as not to cause suspicion as she left the big house. She also insisted Rose not worry about not having any clothes with her, for surely Mr. Granger would take care of her need of a clean dress and undergarments.

Rose desperately wanted to scrub the sooty traveling grime off her body, and from her mind, the haunting picture of her employer pushing his wife down the stairs that troubled her every time she closed her eyes. She wanted a fresh bath, her hair smelling like lavender instead of smoke, and a clean dress to wear instead of one speckled with dust and soot. Surely those requests wouldn't be too much to ask for. Certainly she'd be able to get all those things before she stepped in front of a preacher and married a man she didn't know.

Rose shuddered, glad to have left that big house of death, and the person who caused it. She found herself continuously looking around at other travelers as she journeyed from Wisconsin, then through the Kansas country side. Even now hundreds of miles away she waited for a law man to arrest her, drag her back to testify against a man she now feared. She scoured every face for any indication they were looking for her.

"Next stop, Topeka, Kansas. Passengers going to Dodge City please stay aboard the train, we will only be here long enough to embark and disembark, and take on water."

The train pulled into Topeka, steam from the engine hissing in the air. Rose gazed out the window as the train chugged into town. She tucked her skirts around her, making a protective barrier against anyone who would sit beside her. She'd be glad to finally be rid of the dirt and noise of the wheels churning over the iron rails. To be able to feel the ground solid and unmoving beneath her feet for longer than it took her to use the bathroom to quickly tidy up, a hot bath a simple pleasure she now craved.

A man sporting a star on his lapel sat down across from her. "Ma'am," he tipped his hat and smiled. His eyes were crystal blue. A mustache fell over his upper lip to the corners of his mouth. Rose quickly looked away, her heart pounding. What if he was after her? What if Mr. Griswold forced Abby to tell him where Rose had gone, and he'd hired this man to track her down? Friendly as he may seem, she was afraid that his intense staring would invoke further conversation. She continued to look out the window as the train pulled out of the station. She wanted no conversation with this man, none at all.

"Shouldn't you be getting off here, ma'am?" the man inquired, his easy way of speaking floated over her.

Rose cast him a look, then turned away. She hated being rude to the man. If he wasn't an officer of the law she'd have been happy for a bit of conversation with someone other than herself.

"I don't mean to intrude, but the next stop is Dodge City and I can't suppose a fine young woman like yourself would be traveling there on purpose." The lawman continued to scrutinize her.

Rose sighed, her heart pounding slower in her breast as her fear abated. He didn't know who she was, he wasn't out to drag her back home. It was only too obvious he was not going to give up the gift of gab any time soon.

"Excuse my rudeness, ma'am. My name is Hawkins, Gabe Hawkins. I'm a deputy marshal in Dodge." Deputy Marshal Gabe Hawkins tipped his hat once more, his smile wide and friendly.

"As it happens, I am traveling to Dodge City. I'm meeting my new husband there." Rose chirped, driving home the point that she was already spoken for and not interested in his company.

Hawkins slapped his knee, then laughed. "Well, I'll be dogged! Which one of those Texas cowpokes has decided to take up with a wife all legal like?"

"I don't believe Mr. Granger is a cowpoke." She retorted, disgusted by the fact this man of law thought she looked like she'd marry a dirty cattle runner. "I'll have you know he's a well-respected man in Dodge City."

Deep rolling laughter filled the car. Rose scowled at the deputy, fighting the urge to slap him for his impetuousness. What in the blazes was so funny? Unless, Mr. Granger had lied in his letter...no, that couldn't be. But then she wasn't telling the truth herself.

"Well, that he is ma'am. Well respected by many a man, and woman, in Dodge."

She relaxed at his words. "Good. Now if you'd be so kind as to leave me to my own thoughts, I'd deeply appreciate it." Rose gave him her best sweet smile, then took Mr. Granger's letter yet again from her tattered pocketbook. Unfolding it for the hundredth time, she re-read the words her soon-to-be husband wrote to another woman:

My Dear Miss Johnson,

Thank you for your letter inquiring my advertisement for a bride. As you know, I am in need of a mature woman who knows and understands the running of a household, as well as the needs of a six-year-old girl. That is all I require of you. Rest assured I do not expect you to come all the way from Wisconsin without the promise and protection of marriage.

By your letter, you appear to be perfectly suitable

for my situation. I have provided you with the necessary transportation documents. I hope you have not changed your mind, and I look forward to our joyous occasion upon your arrival.

Respectfully yours,

Logan Granger

Rose fingered the tintype photograph of the man she'd never seen before, but would call husband in a few short hours. His boyish grin only accented the dimples playing on his cheeks. His eyes glittered with a hint of sorrow in their depths. He appeared to have a good head of hair, clean shaven, and well-groomed for a man living in a frontier town. Unless his dress was a lie, Mr. Granger had a sense of fashion.

Nervously she folded the letter with the photograph tucked back safely in its folds. She was a bride on the run. A mail order bride Logan Granger was not expecting at the station.

Logan stood on the depot platform as the Santa Fe finally came to a steamy halt. Smoke from the screeching of steel against steel burst around him.

"Well ole boy, the time has come. I hope you're ready to take on an older sister-type for a wife," Logan said to himself under his breath thankful he was the only one waiting for someone to arrive. It was no secret he was expecting a lady on today's train, he didn't want an audience mulling around that may scare her off. Lilly needed this woman too much. While the future Mrs. Granger may not be physically appealing, he did find himself hopeful she wouldn't have a goiter or warts so he'd be able to look at her and say the words without wincing.

Marshal Jones had come to say his piece. Preacher Samuels was preparing the words he'd recite to the bride and groom over a glass of beer at the Long Branch. Not to mention he had Montana Sue looking after Lilly down at the Lady Gay until he got his new wife to take his name.

Logan sucked in his breath along with his courage. He'd faced down armed men he could do this. The conductor stepped down from one of the passenger cars, followed by an array of men and women from all walks of life. A few looked like city slickers, not unlike he was six months ago, looking for adventure and opportunity. He watched as each person passed by him, and made their way across the street to the hotel. When he looked up again, the prettiest blonde-haired young lady in a plain looking calico dress cautiously stepped down, her skirts gathered in her hand above the dusty street.

Her long hair pulled back in a simple ponytail, pieces of unruly strands fell around her face. She nervously glanced around the platform like a rabbit being cautious of a trap laid out for her. There was a quiet beauty about her that seemed simple and real. What was a young lady like her thinking coming to Dodge City without an escort?

Coming up behind her was Deputy Marshal Gabe Hawkins. Logan's beating heart slowed when Gabe said a few words to the woman, smiled, then made his way over to Logan. Of course, Gabe would pick up a beauty on his travels, it was the way the cards were always laid out for the deputy.

"Logan!" Gabe greeted, his hand extended in friendship. "Good to see a friendly face waiting for me."

"Deputy, looks like you brought a little lady back with you." Logan remarked, surprised at the wave of envy flushing through him. Leave it to Lady Luck, Gabe would get the good-looking girl while Logan waited for his matronly wife-to-be. No time for self-pity, it's what he wanted and embraced when he'd accepted Abigail Johnson's response to his advertisement.

Deputy Hawkins smiled, then burst out laughing. Slapping Logan on the back, he said as he walked away, "She's not with me, Granger. She's here to meet her new husband. Someone named Logan Granger."

Logan swallowed the rock in his throat. His hands were moist and he felt a ping in his britches he'd forgotten existed. His pretty little wife-to-be approached and all he could do was work the brim of his hat over and over in his hands.

For more information or to keep reading, visit my website:
http://maxinedouglasauthor.blogspot.com/p/2012-releases.html

OTHER BOOKS BY MAXINE DOUGLAS

Simply to Die For
Black Horse Canyon Series, Book 1
Romantic Suspense Romance

Leaving one life behind to begin anew, Kandi returns to her home town to open up a candy store. Unfortunately, circumstances pulls her back to the old ways, forcing her to track the trail of a serial porn star killer...

Jimmy, a reporter, discovers the woman he's fantasized about is on the "porn star" killer's hit list. Can he find the killer before the killer finds Kandi?

The Reluctant Bride
Brides Along the Chisholm Trail, Book 1
Western Historical

Rose Duncan hadn't expected the handsome man waiting for her to be a bartender with a six shooter on his hip and a badge on his chest.

Logan Granger hadn't expected his soon-to-be wife to be young, beautiful and a runaway murder witness.

Nashville Rising Star
Contemporary

Utah Sheridan intends to win Nashville Rising Star at all costs; will his bribe be the end of Emerald Braun?

There were only three of them left now—Casey Montgomery from Oklahoma, the darling Emerald Braun, and Utah Sheridan. By this time next week, Utah was banking on only two left standing before the show even started. Emerald Braun wouldn't be one of them. He reached into his pocket and pulled out an envelope. Everything he'd wanted the past few years depends on what's inside it.

Nashville by Morning
Contemporary

Heather Jones is a frustrated writer who falls in love with the southern ways and decides to stay, intending to break into the country music business. James Sheridan is the son of a legendary performer striving to make it on his own. After a breakout song is recorded a Montana storm causes an accident and James leaves the tour bus, and his band, in search of help. Instead he encounters the harsh storm and becomes lost. In a deep depression, Heather retreats to Wisconsin, where she spends months dealing with the probability that her husband will never be found. Will Heather find the peace to move on with her life?

Will James return to find the woman whose memory kept him hopeful of the future and reach Nashville by Morning?

Knight to Remember
Time Travel Romance

In 15th Century England, The Black Knight a/k/a Sir Reynold, has fallen from grace with his childhood friend, Queen Isabel, and is in a no-win situation. He must compete against his friend, and blood brother Thomas. If he wins, Sir Reynold will be banished from Heartsease; if he loses, Thomas will be stripped of his knighthood...

Courtney Parker is a 21st Century seamstress at the Bristol Renaissance Faire. Unlike other reenactors, she performs her profession year-round, making costumes for others. She's always loved the story of the mysterious Black Knight of Heartsease and has looked forward to it every year. But this year's different...

Issie Cummings, the Ren Faire's potion shopkeeper, will stop at nothing to gain what escaped her centuries ago...Sir Reynold Loddington's love and body.

Will Reynold be able to turn back the hands of time and right what went wrong—or will he find himself banned from another country and the woman he loves?

Blood Ties
U.S. Historical Time Travel

A long-lost aunt, two loving ghosts, two people looking for answers, the Civil War and a family legacy all with BLOOD TIES

Emma Sorenson's search for a long lost aunt leads her to

the ancestral home of Royal Kinsman and a path to Civil War.

A story portraying a love so strong that it carries through the Kinsman family from the mid-1860s through generations leading to modern times. Emma travels through three early battles of the American Civil War up to one of the bloodiest days in American history when Royal rescues her at Antietam.

Rings of Paradise
Contemporary Romance

Dear Reader,

I'm not much on putting words to paper, action is more up my alley. I'm Flame, the reigning champion in the Universal Wrestling World (UWW). So why am I here? I grew up in a wrestling family and cut my teeth on the squared circle, which by the way is the only "lady" I trust any more.

I've gone and bought out a small press magazine in Madison, Wisconsin that was going nowhere fast, hired a woman by the name of Khristen Roberts, who according to the editor-in-chief is untrained and wants nothing more than to be a journalist.

Okay, I'm a sucker in helping people out, it's my one weakness, if I have any. Problem is she's on vacation in Hawaii. I've got to catch up with her somewhere along the line for her to join up with me and the UWW. I just hope Khristen is up for the ride...it's always a trip.

Yours truly,
The Flame

The Queen
Seasons of Passion Series Paranormal Romance

Cole Masterson takes a ghost hunting gig aboard the Queen Mary to find out why pictures of his great-grandfather and Hanna Amery are in an old locket.

Hanna Amery finds the love she left behind on The Grey Ghost housed in the body of Cole Masterson, she just needs to figure out how to get to him.

What happens when they find each other on opposite planes of the Universe?

Road Angel
Seasons of Passion Series, Paranormal Romance

Truck driver Lee Thomas believes his life is over after the ghost of his wife who died three years ago steps in front of him and jack-knives his truck on a snowy Wisconsin road on his way home.

Cyn Bedford, an angel, must convince him to fight for his life. She's broken an angel rule and has fallen in love with her charge.

Will Cyn truly be Lee's Road Angel for life?

Eternally Yours
Paranormal Erotica

Cassandra Jameson and her best friend, Paige Matteson, have opened a store in an ancient part of town called

Eternal Pleasures. Cassandra is obsessed with pleasuring herself as no man has ever been able to accomplish, and finds herself an old, tattered book of erotic Victorian tales. She becomes obsessed with a male character which appears in each of the stories she reads and begins to fantasize about him.

Garrett Alexander lived his life performing the teachings of pleasures of the body hundreds of years before. His shop Eternal Pleasures was located in the very same spot that the new Eternal Pleasures has now opened. Having heard the siren call of CJ, Garrett finds he cannot resist the burning desire to pleasure her as no mortal man has ever done before.

Paige Matteson has some promises to fulfill to her best friend...and herself. The mysterious Russell Canterbury may just be the one to take her into a world of sex she'd thought impossible. But Russell has other ideas. He's travelled hundreds of years to seek revenge of CJ for the death of his dear friend, Garrett. Or is it jealousy that spurs him now that Garrett has found peace instead of walking in the shadows of the undead for centuries? What sacrifices are they willing to make for love?

Writing as Debi Wilder

Gabby's Second Chance
Paranormal Erotica

Believing she doesn't deserve to love again, Gabby Adams gets a second chance to find happiness with only one wish. (adult content)

By the Blue Moon
Blue Moon Magic Series, Book 1
Werewolf Erotica

Chastity Langford's thirst for sex is more than just a fascination; it's a coming of age for the wolfen princess. Only she doesn't know why all of a sudden she wants to take the man she loves to hate and roll around on the ground with him. She doesn't understand that this unquenchable thirst is primal and primitive...but she's about to.

Justin Sinclair has waited his entire life for the red-haired girl to grow up. Now that he's been summoned to the United States by Charles Langford to take his rightful place as clan leader, he's looking forward to teaching his betrothed what it means to a wolfen princess.

The coming of the blue moon brings with it dangers to the Alpha clan. Dangers that only Justin and his army can destroy before the Langford princesses are taken prisoner and bred by the Beta leader who destroyed his family.

As Justin battles with his demons on the ground, Chastity wars with her own changes. Having Justin overseeing her moves in her father's company is that last thing she wanted. Bedding him on her terms is one thing, having to work with him is something she didn't bargain for...not even By the Blue Moon.

LETTER FROM THE AUTHOR

Dear Reader,

I hope you enjoyed *The Marshal's Bride*, book 2 of the Brides Along the Chisholm Trail. I have to tell you, I really love the characters of Abby and Gabe. Many readers wrote me asking: "What about Montana Sue, will she finally find the true love she so desperately seeks?" Well, stay tuned as my Brides Along the Chisholm Trail world continues. Montana Sue and Cyrus Kennedy will back in *The Cattleman's Bride* coming soon. Will there be happy endings? Wait and see.

When I was first asked to join the western historical box set, *Wanted: One Bride*, a surge of mixed emotions ran through me. I wanted to do it and was afraid I wouldn't to the genre justice. My wonderful box set and Wednesday morning coffee mates, Callie Hutton and Heidi Vanlandingham, were always encouraging and never once said "then don't do it." I'm so thankful for them believing in me and giving me wings back to Dodge City in 1877.

After I wrote *The Marshal's Bride*, I got so many letters from fans thanking me for the series. As an author, I love feedback. Frankly, you are the reason that I write. So, tell me what you liked, what you loved, even what you hated. I'd love to hear from you. You can write me at maxinedouglasauthor@gmail.com and visit me on the web at http://maxinedouglasauthor.blogspot.com.

Finally, I need to ask a favor, if you're so inclined, I'd love a review of *The Marshal's Bride*. Loved it, hated it, whatever you really think—I'd just enjoy your feedback.

As you might know, reviews can be tough to come by these days. You, the reader, have the power now to make or break a book, or an author. If you have the time to do a review, you can add it to an author's page where you purchased this book as well as other online review outlets.

Please feel free to visit me online. You can find all of my books listed on my blog at http://maxinedouglasauthor.blogspot.com, plus a link to subscribe to my newsletter.

If you are a member of Goodreads, please visit my author page: Maxine Douglas.

If you visit any of my pages, please say "Hello." I'd love to hear from you!

Thank you so much for reading and for spending time with me.

In gratitude,

Maxine

ABOUT THE AUTHOR

Maxine Douglas first began writing in the early 1970s while in high school. She took every creative writing course that was offered at the time and focused her energy for many, many years on poetry. When a dear friend's sister revealed she was contracted to publish a romance it was all Maxine needed to get the ball rolling. She finished her first manuscript in a month's time.

A Wisconsin native, Maxine currently resides in Oklahoma with her husband. While Maxine and her husband may miss their family and friends in the north, they both love the mild winters Oklahoma has to offer. They have established a home in a town southeast of Oklahoma City. They have four grown children, two grand-daughters, two Quarter Horses (mother and son), and a German Shorthair Pointer. And many friends they now consider their OK family.

Maxine is a current member of Romance Writers of America, Oklahoma Romance Writers of America, having served as 2016 President and 2015 President-Elect, and the Wisconsin Romance Writers of American, and EPIC-The Electronic Publishing Industry Coalition.

50361095R00107

Made in the USA
San Bernardino, CA
21 June 2017